going for
broke

BOOKS BY GRETCHEN GALWAY

THE OAKLAND HILLS SERIES

Love Handles (Oakland Hills #1)
This Time Next Door (Oakland Hills #2)
Not Quite Perfect (Oakland Hills #3)
This Changes Everything (Oakland Hills #4)
Quick Takes (Oakland Hills Stories)
Going For Broke (Oakland Hills #5)

RESORT TO LOVE SERIES

The Supermodel's Best Friend (Resort to Love #1)
Diving In (Resort to Love #2)

going for *broke*

an Oakland Hills novel

gretchen galway

ETON FIELD

GOING FOR BROKE

Copyright © 2016 by Gretchen Galway

Cover design: Gretchen Galway
Cover stock graphics: depositphotos.com

Eton Field, Publisher
www.gretchengalway.com

All rights reserved. Except for use in any review, no part of this book may be reproduced or transmitted in any form or by any means, electronic or mechanical, including photocopying, recording, or any information storage and retrieval system, without prior written permission of the Author.

All characters in this book are fictitious. Any resemblance to actual persons, living or dead, is purely coincidental.

ISBN (Paperback): 978-1-939872-15-9
v.20160621

For Mum, who gave me much more than a house.

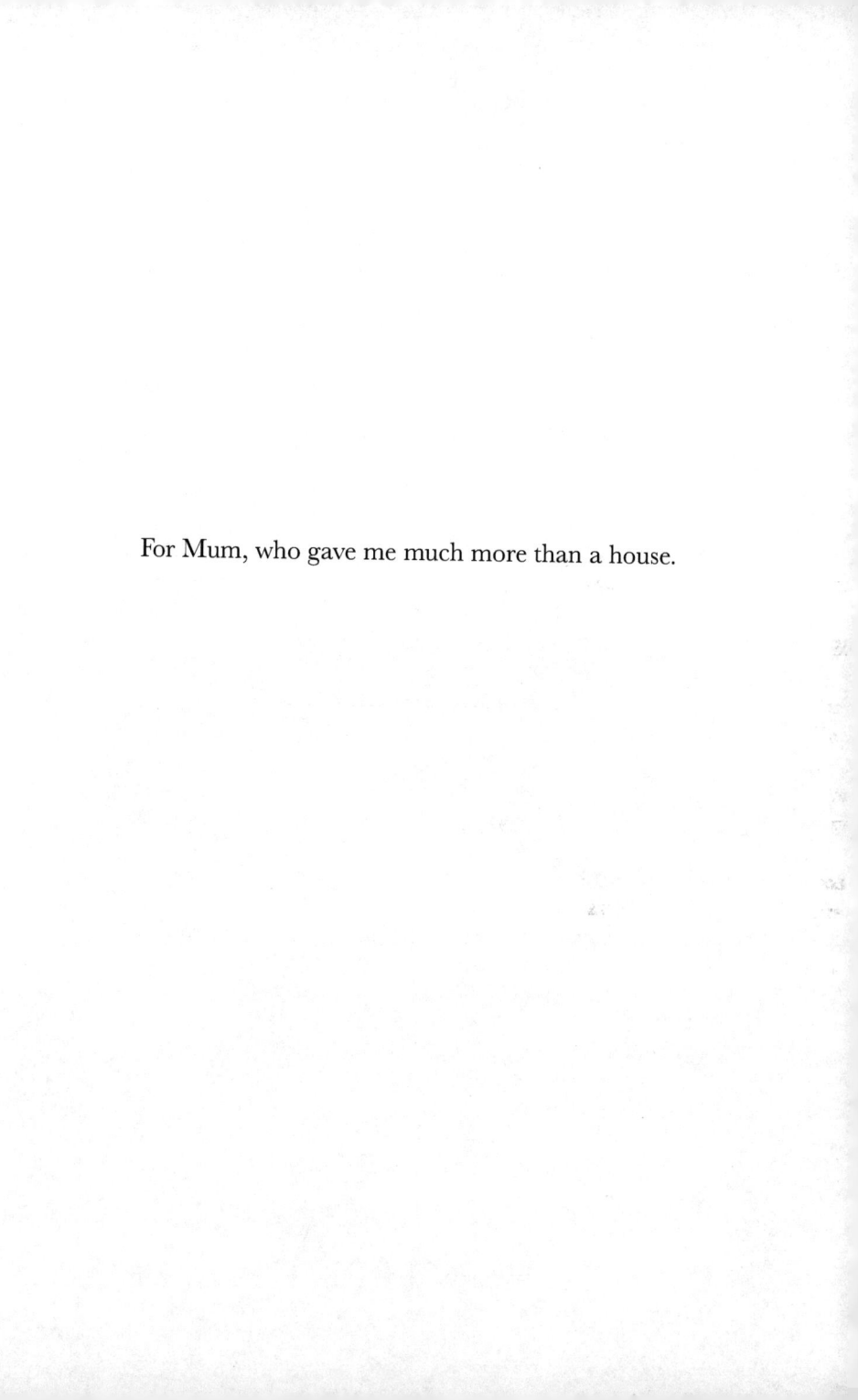

Chapter 1

BILLIE GARCIA WATCHED her ex-boyfriend from across the café, tipping her cup back for another mouthful of Darjeeling before she remembered it was empty.

As empty as her bank account had been when she'd been shacked up with Mr. Right over there last year. His beard was longer now, but well trimmed. It suited him. From the melting looks his female companion was giving him, Billie wasn't the only one to think so.

She squeezed out a few drops from her damp tea bag into her cup. Not for a moment did she regret dumping Josh. He'd bled her dry, financially and emotionally. When she'd told him she was moving out, he'd thought she was kidding. Granted, he was a good-looking guy and she shopped in the big-girl stores, but please. An extravagant, inconsiderate hunk was no prize.

She glanced up at him again, stifling a sigh. If only she'd chosen a different café that morning. Her day had been rough enough without running into her ex. How had she ever fallen for that handsome jerk? Well, yes, he really was handsome. Impossible not to mention it. But was she really so shallow that a pretty face could make her chuck basic standards?

Billie shifted in her seat so that her back was to the couple, then slurped up the dregs of her tea. Maybe she *was* that shallow. She'd allowed that face—and muscles, dimpled chin, and tight butt—to blind her to the obvious.

He'd never loved her. He'd only loved sleeping with her and taking her rent money.

She peeked at the couple again over her shoulder, holding her cup to her lips as a shield. His current victim was a curvy young woman with curly black hair and a trusting look in her big round eyes. A woman who looked suspiciously like Billie—same coloring, hair, body type. He was like a serial killer with a favorite victim profile. She should leave before she gave in to temptation and ran over to warn the poor girl.

When her phone began to ring—and she saw it was her mother—Billie jumped up and quickly left the café without looking back. There were far more important things than exboyfriends.

The sky over Oakland on that February afternoon couldn't decide if it was going to rain or give them a few hours of earlyspring sunshine. Thin raindrops fell from a patchy blue sky onto her A's cap—a hat she was glad she'd been wearing since it had probably stopped Josh from recognizing her. He was horribly nearsighted but had always insisted his generous daily consumption of fermented foods was better than glasses.

At least she hadn't been in love with him. She'd never been that stupid. Not once.

She lifted the phone to her ear and turned away from busy College Avenue to a quiet, residential side street. "Hi, Mom."

"Oh, Billie," her mother, Sandra, said. "How are you doing?" Her voice was pinched with concern.

The grief that Billie had set aside to take a few shallow

moments hating on her ex came flooding back. Just the morning before, her father's mother had died. She'd been ill for some time, and her passing hadn't come as a surprise to anyone, but it was still hard. Billie had loved Grammy to pieces.

"I'm all right," Billie said with a sigh. "I took the day off." She worked in the permit center in the neighboring town of Flores Verdes, just across the bay from San Francisco, and she hadn't been up to another day of taking abuse from a long stream of unhappy citizens. Or her boss.

"You sound like you're outside," her mother said. "I hear traffic. Maybe you should call me back when you get home."

"Why? What is it?"

"It's kind of big news. I want to make sure you can hear me."

Billie stopped in front of a multimillion-dollar bungalow with a tiny yard overflowing with blooming yellow daffodils. Still reeling from Grammy's death, she felt her stomach drop at the thought of another bombshell. "I can hear you. What is it?"

The line went quiet.

"Mom? Are you there?" Billie asked again.

"I'm here. It's just such a surprise. Your father told me ten minutes ago."

"What?" Billie said. "Is it about the cats? Because I'm not allowed to have one where I'm—"

"She left you two the house," her mother said. "Not your father. You and Jane, free and clear. It's yours."

Chapter 2

ALL DAY, BILLIE had been struggling with the realization that she'd never see her grandmother's twinkling gray eyes again.

And now she had to grapple with something else.

"The house in Oakland?" Billie asked.

"What other house is there?"

She could only hope there was another one. Perhaps up in Sonoma County. Or up at Lake Tahoe. A clean, modern, lovely house that wasn't full of cat filth and *People* magazines from the 1980s.

"Me and Jane?" Billie asked. "Why didn't she tell us before?"

"She must've wanted it to be a surprise. She loved you two so much."

Billie's throat tightened. She had trouble getting any words out. "Thanks for letting me know."

"I've upset you. I wanted to tell you before the lawyer did."

"Thanks," Billie said.

"Do call your father. He's having a hard time too."

They'd been divorced for decades, but her parents still talked to one another, perhaps because they'd so quickly moved on to start other families.

"I will." Billie inhaled a calming breath. "After I talk to Jane."

As soon as she got home—a pale shadow of one, since after she'd left Josh, she'd had to sublet a room in a run-down house overflowing with Berkeley students—she called Jane, and the sound of her sister's voice brought all her memories of her grandmother to the surface. They cried for a few minutes, expressing their guilt for not spending enough time with her the past few months, their sadness at her passing, their favorite memories of her over the years.

"I wish she'd told us about the house so we could've thanked her," Jane said.

"I know. It was so generous of her." In her little bedroom, Billie poured filtered water into her electric kettle and turned it on. She drank tea like some people breathed air, but without as many interruptions. "Too bad we'll have to sell it."

Billie had a job, but it was a modest civil service position. Paying property taxes for a single-family home on her salary would be a stretch, let alone paying for all the repairs the place would need. Her sister was a corporate accountant, which meant she had more funds but would be even stingier than Billie was about paying for it all. No doubt they would have to sell it for what they could get and move on.

But Jane surprised her. "Are you kidding?" her sister exclaimed. "This would be a terrible time to sell."

"But the market's up again," Billie said. "We could find somebody who'd buy it."

"You must be out of your mind. Even if we sold it, which we just can't, we'd have to fix it up first. We'd be throwing away a fortune if we didn't," Jane said. "Besides, Grammy left it to us because we'd keep it. If she wanted it sold, she would've given it to Dad. And who knows? Maybe she gave it to us because she felt bad about your renting a room in a house with strangers."

Billie had been too embarrassed to tell either her grandmother or her successful older sister just how bad her current domestic situation was. Six months earlier, she'd left Josh and taken the first thing she could find with a month-to-month lease. Her bedroom was fine, but the communal kitchen violated even the weakest of health codes, so she'd been cooking all her meals in her room with her microwave and electric kettle. And the shared bathroom was even worse. Clods of hair the size of grapefruit huddled like dead animals in the shower drain, leaving her feet standing ankle-deep in a gray, greasy, tepid puddle.

It was still better than living with the wrong guy. Which made her think of Jane's boyfriend.

"Andrew's not going to want to pack up his books and computers and move into Grammy's house," Billie said. "Especially not after he sees it in person."

"Don't worry about Andrew. Even if we don't end up living there, I don't want to sell it. Houses don't grow on trees. Especially so close to San Francisco."

Billie sipped her tea. There were plenty of houses. The problem was they were filled with people who had more money than she did.

"There's nothing like real estate," Jane continued. "Land. A home. Grammy knew how important that was, especially for women. Sure, we have jobs, and food to eat, health insurance. But we won't be able to afford a house like that, not in that location, for a long time."

"I still can't," Billie said.

"I've done the numbers—"

"Of course you have," Billie said. "You eat numbers for

breakfast." Billie preferred scones with extra butter. Way better. But it did explain why she was living in a dump.

"We can split the property taxes fifty-fifty, and the repairs—"

"God knows what else needs to be fixed. Last time I was there, Grammy had duct-taped a crack in the bathroom window. Half the drawers in the kitchen don't slide right. The kitchen floor—"

"Floors are cheap. I'm more worried about the roof and electrical," Jane said.

"You don't *sound* worried."

"We just need to think of it as an investment. One that'll pay off in the best way. I'm so excited." Jane sighed. "And depressed, of course. I'd still rather have Grammy than her house."

"Maybe we should talk about this next week. After the funeral."

"I'll be out of town on business," Jane said. "I'm flying to Chicago on Tuesday for at least a week. I was originally leaving Monday, but my boss is letting me stay for the funeral."

"Nice of her."

"I know, she sucks, but all that corporate money is going to buy us a new roof. Or whatever."

"That's just it, Jane. I don't have any corporate money. I'm a clerk for the lovely but nearly bankrupt City of Flores Verdes, living paycheck to paycheck."

"What happened to your savings? I know you don't take home very much, but a year or two ago you told me you had some tucked away for emergencies. And it's not like you're living the high life."

Billie sipped her tea, her favorite green mint, and felt her face flush with embarrassment. Having known how Jane would never understand squandering money—especially on a man—Billie hadn't told her about the loss of her little savings. "I flushed it down a handsome toilet," she mumbled.

"What?"

"Josh."

Jane gasped. "He *stole* it?"

"Oh no. I gave it to him willingly. I paid the rent, I bought the groceries, I covered his car payment. He was an exotic pet I couldn't bear to give up, like a tiger with a terminal illness, and I had to pay for all his vet bills and special foods." An organic, paleo, gluten-free, grass-fed tiger with bowels even more reactive than his politics.

"But you did give him up finally, thank God."

"Took me too long," Billie said. "Never again."

Jane sighed. "That changes things. I thought you had a nest egg like I do. But if you're broke..." She fell silent.

For a few tantalizing minutes, Billie had gotten caught up in her sister's vision of owning the house and fixing it up. When would they ever get a chance like this again?

"It's not just the money, of course," Jane continued. "We don't know what the place needs. And handling the repairs is going to take more than money. It'll take time. Actually being there, dealing with it all."

That was true. Both of them worked full time. And what did they know about major home repairs? Their mother had hardly been one to pick up a hammer and fix anything. Dad, wonderful though he was, only knew computer hardware, not the other kind, and he'd moved away ages ago. If anything had ever broken at the house, Mom had called her best friend, whose son loved to fix things even though he'd only been a teenager at the time, just like Jane and Billie.

And now he was one of Billie's oldest friends.

An idea began to take shape. A crazy idea, but an irresistible one. Why not take advantage of all the resources they had? Brilliant, industrious, and handsome, Ian Cooper was the peachiest resource around.

Jane would hate the idea. Absolutely hate it.

Billie sipped her tea.

Did her sister really *have* to know all the details? She'd be busy at work. It wasn't as if Billie's friendship with Ian was a secret. Just an unpleasant truth they avoided talking about.

Billie took a deep breath. "My lease is only month to month." She'd been looking around for a new place but hadn't found anything yet. The decent apartments all wanted first and last, a deposit, an animal sacrifice...

Berkeley was impossible in the middle of the school year.

"So?"

"What if I move into Grammy's house?" Billie rushed on. "If you're contributing money, how about I put in the time?"

"You'd do that? Live there in all that mess?"

"If Grammy could do it, why not me?"

"Her sense of smell was long gone," Jane said. "Yours isn't."

"A few gallons of toxic chemicals will take care of that," Billie said. "If I lived there, we wouldn't be in such a hurry to fix everything right away. Without paying rent, I'll be able to contribute more to repairs."

"But we don't know what needs to be done," Jane said.

"Hey, you were the one who wanted to do this."

"I do, I do," Jane said quickly. "Are you really willing to move in? You know what it's like."

"Sure." Grammy's house, as bad as it was, would be like the

Ritz in comparison to where Billie was living now. "You'll be putting in more money than I can. It's only fair."

"That would be great," Jane said. "But don't you want to wait a few weeks before you move in? I'm going out of town. You'll have to tackle the worst of it all by yourself."

Not if Ian agreed to her plan.

"I'm sure," Billie said.

Chapter 3

SEBASTIAN COOPER, KNOWN to everyone as Ian, lifted his screwdriver to the underside of the desk and tightened the plastic hook for holding power cords in place. After a long week of high-stakes financial dealing, he'd jumped at the chance to take a break from staring at a screen.

"Thanks," Lorna said above him. A part-time student at Cal State East Bay, she was his administrative assistant three days a week. "Now there's room for my footrest."

He hunched sideways under the desk and fitted the dangling cords over the hook. "There's an opening here where you can add other cords or move them around if you need to."

"There's more room for my purse and my backpack, too." Lorna leaned down, offering a rare smile. "That's great. Thanks, dude. You're not bad at all."

He was lifting a second hook to finish the job when Lorna stood up and spoke to somebody he couldn't see. "Hi. Who are you?" he heard her ask.

"I've been standing here for five minutes," the man said. "How about you stop flirting with the handyman and tell your boss I'm here?"

Ian froze with the screwdriver in the air. He didn't recognize the voice.

"Actually," Lorna said, warming up for a fight, "this happens to be—"

Ian kicked her in the shin. Smart woman that she was, she fell silent.

"Yeah?" the man demanded.

Lorna, still new to the idea of holding her temper, was slow to reply. "Do you have an appointment?" Her voice was peppered with barely contained rage.

"How about you stop exhausting that little brain of yours and tell the big man that I'm here?"

Ian tapped her shin again, afraid she might knee the guy in the balls. She probably would if he spoke to her like that again. Her feisty temper was one reason he'd insisted that three days a week was her limit. Ian wanted to deal with the visitor in his own way.

"How about you tell me who the hell you are?" Lorna asked, this time in a sickly sweet voice.

"How about I don't. If you don't recognize me, you don't deserve to know."

Ian rolled his eyes. Whoever this guy was, Ian didn't want his money. And that's the only reason the man would be here. Ian's fund had outperformed the market year after year, and if there was one thing rich people wanted, it was to be richer than other rich people.

Maybe it wasn't good for business, but Ian had standards. He'd reached a point where he could pick and choose the people in his life, making decisions that many saw as irrational, even insane. His administrative assistant had anger issues. One of his accountants brought his toddler to work every Friday, preventing many of them from concentrating until the tyke passed out, sticky with apple juice and hummus, under Ian's desk. And his senior analyst couldn't stop herself from singing under her breath. Ever.

Ian liked and trusted his people, and they helped the young firm thrive. What else did he need? So he bought everyone noise-canceling headphones, kept Lorna away from stress, and put a pillow under his desk on Fridays—the cords were safely tied up out of choking range—and tried not to accidentally kick the rug rat in her button nose.

And he was fairly happy. Wasn't that what really mattered? Not that he wasn't rich, too, but he didn't need to be richer than everyone else to hold his head high.

Or duck it under a desk if he felt like it.

Knowing Lorna's patience was already strained, Ian crawled out from under the desk and stood up. He wore his usual loose camp shirt and old khakis on his six-foot-one frame, another advantage of owning his own business. The day he'd opened his office, he'd bagged up all his suits and dropped them off at the community back-to-work center. He'd actually felt guilty about that. Since he'd found them so uncomfortable, why would he be glad to put somebody else in that position? But he wasn't that nuts; he knew an expensive suit could help some needy guy land a great job.

Just not him, not anymore. He had what he'd always wanted.

Well, mostly.

"Whoever you are, get lost," Ian said.

"Are you shitting me?" The man was in his thirties, well dressed (like Ian used to be), and resembled a younger, less-bald Mr. Burns from *The Simpsons*.

Since it was Friday, little Olivia was running around the office with a fistful of baby carrots in a plastic bag. "Watch your language," Ian said. "We've got children around here."

"I'll be nice and pretend I didn't notice," Burns Jr. said, curling his lip.

Ian didn't have time for this. He gave Lorna a look that said she should get back to work, then strode out from behind her desk and approached the visitor with his arms outstretched. "Out," he said, catching him by the shoulder and spinning him around.

"Do you know who I am?"

Ian opened the door. "I don't care."

"I'm worth eight figures."

"Not to me," Ian said. "Out."

The man's eyes widened. He lost some of his swagger. "You're Sebastian Cooper."

"You're leaving."

His tone changed, became overly friendly, ingratiating. "No, listen. Sebastian. Or should I call you Ian?" He smiled, exposing professionally bleached teeth. "I apologize. I didn't realize it was you."

"I don't care." Ian pushed him through the door, shut it between them, and strode back to his own office. "Lorna, please call security downstairs and remind them I don't want any visitors who aren't already on the list."

"Did you see how I didn't even threaten to hit him?" she asked, just before he closed another door, this one to his private office.

He sank down into his recliner and pulled his keyboard into his lap. His monitor hung over him on a mechanical arm he'd designed, allowing him to work while he leaned back, never having to hunch or strain in an uncomfortable posture.

Just as he was lifting his noise-canceling headphones to his head, Lorna knocked and opened the door.

"Hold on," she said. "Don't clock out just yet. You've got company."

"I'm not clocking out, I'm clocking *in*," he said, scrolling through his accounts. The markets were closed for the weekend, but he still had plenty to do. "Tell him you'll call the cops if he doesn't—"

"Not him. That high school girlfriend of yours."

Ian set aside his headphones and keyboard. There was no point in explaining again to Lorna that he'd never dated Billie—only her sister, Jane, who would never, ever visit him—but Lorna clung to her own reality with the tenacity of a terrier. "Billie Garcia's here?"

"I knew you'd want to see *her*."

He gave her a warning look just as Billie's face appeared in the doorway.

"Am I here at a bad time?" she asked.

Chapter 4

IAN SCRAMBLED QUICKLY to his feet. "Of course not."

Lorna let the door bang shut on her way out. She always hurried away in case he asked her to get anything for his visitors.

He walked over to the water dispenser and reached for a cup. "Green tea?" he asked. "I know you avoid the hard stuff after four."

"Green is great," Billie said, smiling. "I can't believe she's still here. Your charming assistant."

Ian glanced up from tearing open a tea bag and was distracted for a moment by the way her dark hair curled around her face. Usually she wore it tied back. He liked it this way, all wild and loose. "I can't fire her. She's too smart."

"Which is why I'm amazed she hasn't quit yet."

"Nobody else would put up with her, and she knows it." He dropped the tea bag into the water and handed her the cup. "What's wrong?"

"Why would something be wrong?"

Crossing his arms over his chest, he perched on the edge of his desk. He never actually sat behind it. That was his old life, and he avoided reminders.

After a long moment, she seemed to realize he wasn't going to say anything more. "Yes, all right," she said. "I was going to call, but I felt awkward. I thought this would be easier. But it's actually harder."

"Go into the hall and call me from there. I'm easy."

She grinned, dimples forming in each cheek. Superficially, she and Jane, the older sister he'd dated, could've been twins. But when she smiled, Billie's face became entirely her own: playful and fun. Chronically immersed in his work, which was all numbers and stress, he enjoyed Billie's warm, easygoing company whenever he could get it. A drink after work, weekend hikes on Mt. Tam, sharing the drive up to visit their mothers, going dutch for a night of stand-up comedy, which they both loved.

"Did you hear my grandmother died?" Billie asked.

His pleasure faded. "No. I didn't. I'm sorry."

"Last Thursday. I thought your mom might've told you."

Their mothers up in Sonoma County, where they both grew up, got together at least once a week. "She left me a message, but I haven't called her back yet."

"I know how that is," she said, flashing a dimple. But then her face suddenly crumpled and she looked away.

He held his breath. Emotions weren't his strong suit.

"I'm sorry," she said, smiling in that funny way people do when they're trying to hold it together. "It just hit me again. I'm a mess."

The thought of seeing Billie cry unnerved him. She was the happiest person he knew, quick with a joke or a self-deprecating smile. Nothing ever seemed to faze her. She always bounced back, slow to complain about her troubles even when she had plenty: at school, at work, with money, with men.

But they didn't discuss her love life, or his. It was the one topic they carefully avoided.

They had to. Neither one of them could ever forget the years he'd been involved with her sister. It had been over ten years now, but high school sweethearts weren't like other couples. You didn't forget. You couldn't. Even if you wanted to.

Taking away her cup of cheap, tepid tea, he took her by the shoulders and ushered her into his recliner. "You've had a hard day. Take a minute." He moved away and dumped the cup into the trash.

Leaning forward to get out of the chair, Billie wiped her eyes and shook her head. "No, no, I'm fine—"

Gently but firmly, he pushed her back into the chair. "Take a minute," he repeated, then marched out into the main office, where he found Lorna painting her toenails.

"I need you to get some tea at the café," Ian told her. "Something rare and expensive that normal people have never heard of."

Lorna scowled at her toe but nodded. By now she'd learned which moments were important, those moments when he was the boss. "Anything for you?"

"No, but you can get yourself something too." He handed her a twenty, paused, added several more. "And whatever else people want," he said, waving at the rest of the team as he returned to his office.

"I could buy a pony with this," Lorna called after him.

He closed the door. Billie's tears were gone, but her expression was still bleak.

"I'm really fine—" she began.

"Put these babies on," he said, reaching over her to the second platform he'd built to hover over his chair, which held his earphones, tablet, beverage, phone, and other sundries. He picked up the earphones and slipped them over her head, fluffy curls and all. They were soft and springy, and he tried not to inhale the scent of her shampoo or anything else. When he clicked the switch over her ear, her face lit up.

"Ooh, everything got quiet," she said loudly. "These are the expensive ones."

He nodded.

"But I can still hear things," she said. "It's just muffled."

With his bare toe—he wore flip-flops, as he usually did—he lifted the seat under her calves, seesawing her backward into a relaxing, supine position. The buttery leather over memory foam and teak was sure to soothe her more effectively than any awkward words about grief, loss, and the cycle of life. Not that he'd ever be able to come up with any words like that without a week to prepare.

He switched on the heated massage.

When she closed her eyes, moaning, no longer trying to sit up, he retreated to his desk in satisfaction. Sitting on the edge again, he watched her as she sighed and sank deeper into his chair. As he often did, he tried to see any resemblance between the two sisters and their mother. Sandra had straight blond hair and a lean, angular body like a marathoner. Billie and Jane, both brunettes, were curvy all over.

His gaze was exploring those curves when Lorna burst in with the tea. With pierced eyebrow raised, she glanced at Billie before handing him the cardboard tray. Feeling his face heat, he took it from her, annoyed, and waved her away. She rolled her eyes and smirked as she sauntered out.

Billie had opened her eyes and was watching him. The bulky, rounded earphones gave her a cute Princess Leia look.

"Here," he said gruffly, walking over with the cup held out to her.

She slipped off the earphones and took the tea with both hands. "You didn't have to do that."

"But Lorna did. Every once in a while, I have to remind her who's boss."

Inhaling the steam wafting up from the cup, she smiled. "Well, thanks, but I'm fine. I didn't mean to get weepy. I thought I was OK by now." She tipped the seat forward, momentarily unbalanced, and he reached out to steady her. Her puffy vest deflated under his fingers and he felt her soft, warm shoulder.

"Don't get up," he said. "There's no hurry."

"But—"

He picked up the remote control for the chair and turned up the massage. "Relax. Tell me why you came by."

He knew it couldn't be for grief counseling. People didn't come to him with emotional problems, only financial and mechanical ones.

She looked into her cup. "Now that I'm here, I think I was stupid to even think of it. I'm sorry. I forget you're such a big shot now. Because I've known you so long, I'll always think of you as the guy who came over to fix the plumbing. Not the world-famous financial guru."

"I'm neither world famous nor a guru."

"Close enough." She smiled and lifted her tea, her dimples flashing.

His mind began to process the clues. "Did you need some help with her house?"

Her jaw dropped. For a full second, she stared at him. "How the heck did you figure that out?"

"Just being logical. She just died, and now you're here talking about plumbing. I remember you saying she lived in Oakland." When she continued to gape at him, he added, "Did you inherit the house?"

Her jaw dropped another inch, flashing him a view of her tonsils. "Me and Jane. How could you possibly guess that? It was a total shock."

"Because you're here," he said. "If she'd left it to your dad, he'd be taking care of it."

Eyes wide, she shook her head. "This is why they pay you the big bucks. You're supernatural."

"Just good at putting together the details."

"Right. That's all," she said.

"Is the house in bad shape?"

She nodded. "It's going to need a lot of work, but we don't know exactly what." Lifting the cup to her lips again, she mumbled, "I had this idea that you could walk through the house and take a look. You've always been handy. And Jane and I are so *not*."

The room fell silent as he thought it over.

Jane wouldn't want his help. Their breakup had been awkward. He wasn't crazy about seeing her again, but it didn't bother him as much as it seemed to bother her.

"It seemed reasonable before I got here," she said, climbing out of the chair. "But now I can see it's too much to ask. We'll need to hire a pro."

He shook his head, lost in his thoughts. An old house in need of major repairs was a tantalizing thought. All that work would be satisfying in a way that tying up electrical cords—and even making money—could never be.

And he liked Billie. He'd always regretted that his long hours at work didn't allow for much social life. "Hold it."

"No, forget it," she said. "Thanks again for the tea. I'm sorry to bother you. You probably lost a billion just taking the time to see me."

She was across the room and reaching for the doorknob before he snapped out of it and jogged over. He put his back on the door, blocking her way, and looked down at her. "What about Jane?"

"I told you, forget it. I know you hate to see each other."

"Jane might," he agreed. "But I don't mind."

Billie pressed her lips together for a moment. "Honestly, I wasn't going to tell her. I thought we could be sneaky." Then she smiled, devilish but cute. Nobody could look evil with dimples like that.

He found himself smiling in return. "Give me the address."

Chapter 5

BILLIE WONDERED WHY she'd come to see Ian in person. If the phone had seemed too awkward, why not an email, for God's sake?

Her grandmother's funeral on Monday had been short and bittersweet, just a simple ceremony and reception that had brought everyone in the family together for a day.

And then they'd all split apart again, returning to their everyday lives. Jane had flown to Chicago, and each day since, Billie had meant to ask Ian about helping with the house. It had taken her until today to get up the nerve.

She took a step sideways and looked down at her cup, breaking the eye contact between them.

He'd always had a way of staring at you with those piercing blue eyes that felt like the NSA was sifting through your deepest secrets. Probing, analytical, ruthless. The brain that had gotten him into MIT and into the ranks of the one percent before his twenty-fifth birthday would, occasionally, become interested in human beings instead of finance. And when that happened, he was better than the most empathetic, fuzzy-brained psychotherapist.

But when he smiled...

It was worse. Much worse. He was much too good-looking for his own good. Or hers, anyway.

"She was a hoarder," Billie said. She suddenly wanted to scare him away. "The house is filled with garbage. God knows what needs to be fixed—the roof, the foundation, the electrical. We should just sell it and—"

"I'll take a look," he said. He took out his phone and tapped his screen. "I was flying to New York tomorrow, but I can change that. I can be at the house first thing in the morning, eight or nine. We can—"

"Hold on, you don't have to cancel anything." She'd forgotten how intense he could be when he set his mind on something.

"It's not a big deal. I'm glad to have a reason not to go." He went back to his phone. "Is eight too early for you?"

"In the morning?" Just thinking about getting up that early on a Saturday made her yawn.

But if he was willing to do a walk-through, she could hardly turn him down. Even if it was at an ungodly hour. "Sure, of course," she said. "That would be fantastic."

His hawk-like features warmed into a grin. "Fantastic," he said, turning and opening the door. "I can't wait."

...

Can't wait, he'd said.

Thinking about Ian's words, Billie pulled her car into her grandmother's driveway at eight the next morning. *Her* driveway. What an oddly powerful feeling. She'd never owned property before and discovered the sensation was surprisingly awesome. Even if she had to get up before noon on a Saturday.

She'd been to the house on the day of the funeral, but this was different. Her plethora of relatives weren't here to distract her.

Her family was enormous and complicated; the term "blended" didn't do it justice. Both of her parents had been married twice, with each marriage producing two children, and she'd given up trying to explain it to people without drawing a diagram.

Grammy had been her father's mother, but most of the blended clan, even Billie's mother and Billie's younger half sisters, had come to the funeral pay their respects. Clara Garcia, her grandmother, had been eccentric but sweet, lavishing love on her family, even her ex-daughter-in-law, whenever she wasn't too absorbed with her cats.

Oh, the cats. This morning, studying the house from her car, Billie worried about how Ian would react to the mess her grandmother's animals had left behind. Aunt Trixie, her dad's cousin, had taken one of them and found a home for two more. A neighbor, apparently, had taken a fourth. A fifth, sadly, had been put down just a week before Grammy had gone into hospice care.

Five was a lot of cats for anyone, but especially for an eightysomething woman who had never, even in youth, been an organized, tidy person. The walker and oxygen tank made daily animal maintenance almost impossible.

If only she hadn't been so adamant about refusing help.

Billie climbed out of her secondhand Hyundai and gazed at the house. It was from what they now called "midcentury," but her mother affectionately called "*fifties fugly.*"

"Hello there," a man's voice called out from her right. "Are you Jane?"

She turned to see a man about her age in a sweatshirt and jeans, approaching from the yard next door, holding a cat. Both he and the cat were sandy-haired.

"No," she said warily, because this wasn't the middle of Kansas, it was Oakland. "Who are you?"

"Then you must be Belinda," he said, shifting the cat to the other arm, stepping over the hedge, and walking to her side. He had vivid blue eyes, a pierced ear, and a body that was either genetically gifted or carefully constructed in a gym.

"Who are you?" she repeated. She didn't like strange men, even the hot-bodied ones, to get so close when she was alone in a strange place. At her job, working with the rudest members of the public had taught her how to be cold and warm at the same time. Extra cold when necessary.

"Oh, sorry," he said, lifting his hand in a motionless wave. "Todd."

That didn't quite cover all the bases. But she didn't really want to know anything else about him; she was eager to get inside. With a faint smile, she nodded and moved to walk up to the front door.

"I'm the one who adopted your grandmother's cat," he said.

Chagrined, she turned. "I'm sorry. I didn't realize. Thank you." She studied the animal in his arms but didn't recognize it.

"Not this one," he said. "She's inside."

"How many do you have?"

"Only the two," he said. "Mine and your grandmother's. When Clara was having trouble, I figured it was the least I could do. She was a nice lady."

"Thank you," she said again, trying to warm up to him a little. "Well, it was nice to meet you, Todd."

"You are Belinda, right?"

"Everyone calls me Billie."

He smiled. "Clara talked about you." He stroked the cat

behind the ears. A tattoo of a leafless tree decorated his wrist, its black branches winding around his forearm. "I work at home, so I saw her a lot. She told great stories."

"Yeah, she did," Billie said, smiling sadly.

"Well, I'll let you go. I just wanted to introduce—"

At that moment, Ian's black pickup pulled into the driveway.

Chapter 6

BILLIE WAVED AT Ian, relieved to see him, and turned to Todd. "Thanks for coming by. And for taking in her cat."

Todd's eyes were fixed on Ian, who was stepping out of the pickup. "You know this guy?"

"I know this guy," she said.

Todd was still standing there when Ian reached them with a bag slung over his shoulder and two steaming Starbucks cups in his hands.

"Morning," Ian said, handing a cup to Billie. Tea bag labels on strings flapped in the breeze.

Smart man. He knew better than to bring her coffee.

Billie moved to Ian's side, edging closer to the house. "This is Todd, a neighbor. Todd, this is Ian," she said quickly. "Well, we should be going."

"Nice cat," Ian said to Todd.

Todd's eyes narrowed. "He doesn't like strangers."

There was an awkward pause.

Ian looked at Billie. "I got you tea."

"I know," she said, holding it up with a smile. "Thank you."

Without a word, Todd turned, jumped over the hedge, and strode up the front steps of the little white bungalow next door.

"Well, see you later," Billie called after him. "Thanks again."

If Todd responded, she didn't hear him.

Ian followed her up the stairs to the front door, which she opened with the keys her father had given her at the funeral. The immediate family had met at the house for a few minutes after the service, but because of its condition, they'd immediately relocated to Jane and her boyfriend's apartment near Lake Merritt instead.

"Know that guy long?" Ian asked, too polite to mention the cat stench wafting down the hallway.

"Just met him a few minutes ago."

"Weird," Ian said.

For some absurd reason, his comment made Billie want to defend Todd, even though he'd given her the creeps too. "Just because he likes cats?"

"I like cats. Doesn't mean I've ever walked around with one."

"He took in one of my grandmother's cats," she said.

"That one?"

"No. He said it was inside." She shivered and went over to the thermostat, an ancient circular device on the wall surrounded by family photos.

"I wonder why he didn't bring that one out to show you," Ian said. "Instead of the one that didn't like strangers."

She twisted the thermostat and heard a click, then a roar, as the furnace turned on. "Grammy liked to keep the house warm, so at least the heating should work."

But Ian, apparently, was still thinking about the neighbor. "Maybe he killed it."

She tried to express shocked disapproval. "It was nice of him to take it in."

"And then ate it," Ian added.

Billie broke out laughing. "God, he was weird, wasn't he?" Maybe she was getting better about good-looking guys ruining her judgment. She hadn't been even remotely tempted to flirt with Todd, not even for a second.

After flashing her a grin, Ian slipped the bag off his shoulder and started to set it on the grimy floor before seeming to think better of it and hanging it on the closet doorknob. "She had a lot of cats, I take it?"

"We tried to help her with the mess, but she wouldn't let the cleaners inside. Only family."

"And Todd, apparently," he said.

"I doubt it. They probably did all their chatting outside. Going out for the paper and the mail was her big excursion of the day. She'd push her walker down the driveway, greet the neighbors, wave at people jogging to the park, pet everyone's dogs, talk to the UPS guy, and if she didn't see anyone, she'd wait. Her walker had a little seat on it. She'd perch there and hang out."

Feeling an intense urge to go out and talk to her that very minute, Billie held her breath, blinking back tears.

"She sounds like a nice woman," Ian said. "I wish I'd met her."

"She was awesome. Please don't get the wrong idea when you see the house. It was just the one thing she couldn't handle. Everyone has their thing, right?" Smiling, she sniffed.

"At least one." He pulled a square of white fabric out of his jeans pocket and held it out to her.

She took it and stared at him. "You carry real handkerchiefs around?"

"My mother," he said. "She gives me a few every Christmas. They've uh, got my initials on them." He cleared his throat and stood up taller, looking embarrassed.

Amused, she looked down, patting her eyes with the handkerchief, reluctant to actually blow snot into a monogrammed gift from his mother.

Something brown formed an L-shaped smear on the ex-beige carpet. Perhaps in the previous century—the middle of it—the material had been as light and fluffy as a newborn baby's stuffed animal. But now the fibers were ground into a stained, patchy, clumpy mass, more like a skin disease than a fabric. "I snuck a vacuum cleaner in with me once while she was napping, and she got so mad she wouldn't let me in again for a month."

Ian turned and went over to the corner near the front door, where he squatted down and began tugging at the edge of the carpet. It made popping sounds as he peeled it back. "Good news," he said. "You've got excellent hardwoods under here."

She walked over. "Really? My dad said it was probably just cheap subfloor."

"I don't know about the rest of the house, but here you've got hardwoods. They'll need some work, but they'll be an improvement over... this." He plucked at the scabby carpet. "Whatever this is."

She leaned over his shoulder to get a better look at the planks under the row of rusty nails and splintered plywood strips. "Fantastic," she breathed, squeezing his shoulder, imagining all the work his big muscles could do. "Let's pull it all up right now."

He turned his head, bringing his nose close to her cheek. "Now? It's usually best to do the floors last."

Another shiver, not from cold, ran through her. She'd always been smart about keeping casual around Ian. Their mothers were friends, they were friends. They'd grown up together, or as much as you can when you're three grades apart.

Although there *had* been that moment when she was twelve and she'd noticed the way his raven-black hair brought out the bright summer-sky blue of his eyes, and that he was as big as a man and looked more... interesting... in jeans than other guys did.

She'd noticed.

But when her sister announced that she and Ian were "going out" (although sometimes they stayed in doing things only grown-ups should do), Billie worked hard at not noticing anything more about him. Especially not the good things, such as how he was brilliant and ridiculously nice, even when she was throwing Doritos and making smooching noises from behind the couch.

Years later, when he'd broken up with her sister and they were all out of school, and Jane living in LA, Billie had been glad to become friends with him. Carpooling up to see their mothers, she'd thought he seemed lonely and isolated, without much of a life outside work, even after he'd quit the corporate grind and started his own company. She'd always thought it was good for him to hang out with a normal person like her, who had some college but no degree, a full-time job but no money.

Hang out. Not *go out* or *stay in*.

Friends.

Straightening quickly, she turned her attention to the job at hand. And not his hands, which were tanned and attached to well-muscled forearms.

"I'd love to do it now, but we probably shouldn't," he said.

Swallowing a smile, she nodded. *Definitely shouldn't.*

"Let me show you the rest of the house," she said.

Chapter 7

IAN GOT TO his feet and watched Billie walk away. She wore tight jeans and a short black hoodie, nothing particularly unusual or evocative, but he found himself staring at her butt longer than he should have.

Wafting cat odor reminded him of where he was and whose body he was admiring. Getting to his feet, he brushed off his knees—something sticky clung to his palms afterward, so he had to brush those off as well—and followed Billie down a hallway into a dark room at the back.

"Could you help me? She never opened these." Billie was tugging at the heavy curtains covering everything from floor to ceiling. Not a hint of light broke through from outside.

After tripping over something on the floor, he took out his pocket flashlight and flicked it on. Around them crowded heavy furniture and piles of stacked boxes as tall as he was.

"Technically, this is the living room," she said. "She never used it, though. She always kept the door closed. I've been dying to know what it really looks like." With a grunt, she continued to pull at the curtains.

Aiming his flashlight over her head, he saw the way the drapes were attached. "Hold it. They're nailed to the wall."

Billie stopped and let out a loud sigh. "Oh, Grammy. Seriously?"

"I'll get my gear. Just a second." He returned a few minutes later with his hammer and a small crowbar. "Think there's a ladder around here?"

"I've never seen one. Maybe in—"

"Never mind. See if you can find a working lamp," he said. "I'm going to get my ladder out of my truck."

When he got back, she'd dragged a light in from somewhere and was pointing it at the curtains. "I can't believe she nailed them. She must've done that ages ago, before she hurt her hip." She paused. "Is that duct tape?"

He set up the ladder and climbed up to where she was pointing. "Afraid so." In a few minutes, he'd removed six nails and torn away three layers of tape, freeing the corner of the curtain so that a beam of bright morning sun streamed in. Dust motes floated in the light, shimmering like fireflies.

Billie sneezed.

"There are masks in my bag," he said. "Help yourself."

"I'll be all right."

"I insist," he said. "And please get me one too."

Wearing their low-budget hazmat equipment, they removed dozens of square yards of thick, dusty, mildewy fabric. Each inch encouraged them to go faster, because they were revealing a stunning, sunny view of San Francisco, the bay, the Golden Gate Bridge, Alcatraz, and the slopes of the East Bay hills around them. The world outside was much more appealing than the one inside.

"Guess she didn't like the view," he said.

"She was afraid of heights." Billie had both hands pressed up against the glass and was peering out in wonder. "Look at the yard. Well, what used to be a yard."

He looked down into a flat, wide plot of weeds, cardboard boxes, plastic tubs, a tangled web of rusty bicycles, and the ruins of a broken swing set, now slanted at a forty-five degree angle and overrun with ivy. "It's huge for up here. And level. Most of the houses along here don't have nearly so much usable land."

"She used it, all right. As a landfill." Her voice was bleak.

"No big deal. One debris box and some muscle, and it'll be beautiful." He put a hand on her shoulder. "Take a break outside and I'll go through the rest of the house."

"What? No, I'm fine. I was just wishing…" She put a hand over his and leaned against him. "I wish I could've done this while she was alive. Now she won't be able to appreciate it. It's too late —" Her voice cracked, and she fell silent.

"Come on." He grasped her arm and led her out of the house to the sunny front step, where bright flowers were spilling out of a dozen small pots. The front of the house, unlike the back, was clean, happy, and tidy.

"Deep breath," he said, inhaling one himself. "It's toxic in there."

"Which is why I can't subject you to it another second." She pulled her hand free and turned to go back into the house. "I'll get your ladder and your bag, and you can go. I'm so sorry to put you —"

"I'm having a great time," he said, and it was true. The thought of cleaning out the decrepit old house filled him with an excitement he hadn't felt since he'd landed his first multimillion-dollar investor. "Don't worry about me."

She stared at him. "Really?"

"This place is going to be beautiful when I'm done with it."

"When *you're* done with it?" She laughed and tore the mask off her head, shaking off bits of debris. Some remained in her hair, which bothered him, and he had to fight the urge to run his fingers through each strand and make it as glossy and voluminous as it had been before.

He shoved his hands in his pockets. "You don't want my help?"

"Ian, you've got a company to run. You don't have time to fix up my grandmother's house."

"I have plenty of time."

"I was grateful you came today just to eyeball the place. That's more than enough."

"Hardly. You can't do this by yourself," he said.

"I've got my sister."

"I bet Jane works longer hours than anyone I know. And that's saying something."

The white dust mask cupped her chin, emphasizing her rosy cheeks. Her brow was furrowed. "You can't mean it. You've seen what it's like in there," she said. "We haven't even looked at the outside yet. Jane's worried about the roof."

He reached past her and tapped his knuckles on the drainpipe. It was solid, and he didn't see any sign of soil erosion along the house below the gutter. The exterior windows were clean, too, and the sycamore arching over the front had been recently trimmed. The mulch around the shrubs and perennials was freshly raked and weed-free. "I suspect you'll find that most of the repairs will be on the interior."

"Why do you think that?"

"Look around," he said, gesturing at the garden, the clean steps, the shining glass windows. "Did you or your sister or your dad have the trees trimmed?"

"Trees?" She frowned up at the branches.

"If your grandmother was afraid of heights, I doubt she was the one who climbed up there."

"Not to mention she was on oxygen and needed her walker. If she'd climbed up there, I would've been right down here making a video."

"There you go. She must've hired somebody," he said.

"So what if she did?"

"Then she probably hired people for the roof, too." He took out his phone and pulled up his note-taking to-do app. "I'll call for a pest inspection. And I know an electrician who can check out the wiring." He began jotting down a checklist.

"Ian."

He continued to type. Lorna must know some strong guys at school who'd like to make a few bucks hauling the garbage out of the house. Which would mean he'd have to order a debris box. He made another note.

"*Ian.*"

"There's no point arguing, Billie. I'm here, I'm on the job. Don't waste your energy trying to get rid of me. You'll need all of it for what lies ahead."

Chapter 8

BILLIE WAS OPENING her mouth to argue again when a baby-blue Volt turned in to the driveway. Inside was an older lady with short hair and a big smile.

Trixie? "What's she doing here?" Billie asked under her breath.

"Who is she?"

"One of my dad's cousins. We call her Aunt Trixie." Billie waved at the figure walking toward them. If Trixie hadn't been at the funeral, she probably wouldn't have recognized her. The two family branches knew each other but had drifted apart. "Grammy was her mother's sister."

"I hope I'm not interrupting," Trixie said, glancing between them. "Your sister told me you were here."

"Is something wrong?" Billie asked.

"Well, your grandmother died." Trixie reached out and squeezed Billie's arm. "I'm so sorry."

"Thank you." Billie offered an awkward smile. Her father, being more than ten years younger than his cousin, hadn't known her very well, and Billie couldn't think of why she'd come over. "You live here in Oakland, don't you?"

"Not far at all. Which is why I wanted to come by and see if I could help. I know what it can be like after a death. You must be overwhelmed." Trixie's gaze turned to Ian and brightened. "But you've got big, strong, handsome help already. How wonderful."

"You can help me convince her of that," Ian said. "She seems to think she can do it on her own."

"I'm sure she's just being polite." Trixie walked past them and reached for the front door. "How about we go inside? The neighbors are staring."

The neighbors? Billie looked up at the house next door and saw Todd watching them from an upstairs window. "All right, that's just creepy."

"He's probably lonely," Trixie said, holding the door open for them. "I'm sure Clara told him about you and Jane. The women in our family can't resist pairing up the young people. My own mother was the same way."

Billie glanced up at Todd again. As they went inside, Ian leaned over and made a strangled cat sound in her ear. As if it were being eaten.

"I'm afraid it's a mess," Billie said, running a hand through her hair. Trixie might have been family, but she felt embarrassed for her grandmother's sake. The Garcia branch of the family wasn't well represented by the feline decrepitude currently on display.

"It just got too much for her, poor thing," Trixie said. She didn't recoil at the smell or express shock at the worn carpet, the piles of papers, the stacked boxes everywhere. "The mail and the newspapers and the mail-order packages, coming day after day, all of it needing to be sorted and chosen and rejected. And so much waste in the world and you don't want to contribute to it, but to fix and reuse and recycle everything is just too much work. Poor Clara. After a while, she probably couldn't see it the way we do."

"That's what I was telling Ian," Billie said, relaxing a little.

Maneuvering around piles of boxes, Trixie marched through the house like a real estate agent on a deadline, flipping light switches and checking the plumbing, kicking cabinet doors, peering into closets, admiring the view they'd uncovered out the back room. "You've got a lovely house here. How wonderful you've got a handy friend to help you out."

Billie glanced at Ian, who smiled.

"I'm sure the last thing you can imagine wanting right now is furniture," Trixie continued, "but I've recently acquired a man who has a house full of it. We've been trying to get our children to take it, but they've got homes of their own or different tastes, or maybe they just don't want their stepfather's things because it's kind of weird. Anyway, we've got loads. It's yours if you want it."

She vaguely remembered meeting Trixie's new husband at the funeral. Although he'd seemed like a cool guy, the thought of taking in an older man's furniture wasn't one of her real estate fantasies, unless that older man was Ralph Lauren or something. But she was practical; she knew she couldn't afford to be picky. "Maybe, yes. Thanks. I'm not sure yet what we'll need."

"From what I can see, you'll need to get rid of everything of your grandmother's." She offered a sad smile. "The cats, you see."

"Yeah, the cats." Billie sighed.

"Even if you refinish the scratches, there's still the smell," Trixie said.

In unison, the three of them sniffed. And then coughed.

"It really is impressive," Ian said. "We might have some trouble if it's soaked into the floorboards."

Trixie patted his arm, beaming up at him. "You'll figure it out." She looked at her wrist. "I've got to be going. I'll be in touch.

You let me know about Hugo's furniture. Take it from me, his bed is fantastic. Definitely a keeper." Winking at Ian, she turned on her heel and floated out of the house, dodging the garbage, and slammed the front door behind her.

"That's nice," Billie said into the stinky darkness, although the morning wasn't going as smoothly as she'd hoped. They still hadn't looked at the big things Jane had mentioned—electrical, plumbing, foundation, roof. "I'll probably need to take her up on that furniture. I can't afford to be too proud."

"Precisely," Ian said, pulling out his phone. "Which is why you're going to let me do what I can do and not fight me."

"I just don't understand why you'd want to," she said.

"Making money only goes so far."

"Really? I'd think it would go way past this," she said, smiling. "Like by several million light-years."

"How many sets of keys do you have to the house?"

She pulled them out. The keychain was a neon-orange stuffed cat as big as her fist and played a mechanical "meow" if you rattled it. It was rather fantastic. She was definitely keeping it. "Just the one."

Without touching the cat, Ian caught the ring between his fingers and freed the two brassy keys. "I'll make a copy and get them back to you. It'll take me a few days to clear my schedule, but we can meet here same time next week."

"Hold on, I need those."

"We can't do much more here until we haul out the garbage. I'll also get one of those storage pod things so you can move the uncategorized items into it—mementos, valuables, charity stuff, that sort of thing. That way you don't have to decide everything all at once."

This was a side of Ian Cooper she'd heard about but never seen for herself—the take-charge, dominating side. It was kind of cute. Even sexy. He probably talked that way in bed.

But she wasn't going there. She reached out to reclaim the keys but inadvertently knocked the keys to the matted ex-carpeting.

"I need those," she said, bending over to retrieve them. "I'm moving in here later today."

"Moving what in?"

"Myself. My stuff."

"No, you're not."

"I am," she said. "I've already given notice. Another guy moves in Wednesday." Because she'd been subletting, she didn't have any furniture to move. Trixie's offer had been even more helpful than she knew. What little she'd had, she'd already sold to cover the rent. Living with her ex-boyfriend had been expensive, and moving out suddenly last year had demanded sacrifices.

"Where are you going to sleep?" Ian asked.

"I think I'll put my bed down in the kitchen. It's the one room she kept relatively clean." It was only a blow-up air mattress, so it would be easy to move around.

He scowled. "You mean you're actually going to sleep inside the house? You won't be able to smell anything for a month. Why not stay at Jane's if you have to?"

"Jane lives with her boyfriend. There's no room for me."

"I'm sure you could crash on the couch for a few days," he said.

Billie couldn't believe she was arguing with him. They never argued. "The whole point is I can take care of things personally by being here when I'm not at work."

He stared at her, waved the fist holding the keys. "I should hold on to these to save you from yourself. At least until I've cleaned out the litter boxes."

"You are *not* touching my grandmother's cat shit," she said. "That's a bridge too far, buddy. We've been friends for a long time, but it's not like I took a bullet for you in a war or something. You don't owe me anything."

"I told you. I enjoy this. Making order out of chaos is one of the great pleasures of my life."

"I thought making mountains of cash was your great pleasure."

He shrugged. "Everyone needs a hobby."

Well, damn. He really wanted to do this. How could she turn him away? Who was she to stop a tall, handsome guy from strapping on a tool belt and going to work on her?

On her house. Her house.

Reality kicked in. She was Jane's sister. Jane who was his ex-girlfriend, Jane who was her closest sister and best friend, Jane who would be uncomfortable to know he'd even stepped over the threshold.

"Jane won't like it," Billie said.

He shrugged. "Don't tell her."

"I have to."

"You didn't today," he said.

"That was one time for a quick walk-through. And I already feel guilty."

He crossed his arms over his chest. "All right. Tell her. It's your house too. Do you plan on getting permission from her every time you want to have somebody come over?"

"No. Only before you do." She rolled her eyes. "For obvious

reasons."

"You and I are friends. You'll be living here now. Jane and I are bound to run into each other more often from now on." His expression hardened. "If she has an issue seeing me, that's her problem."

Billie couldn't tell him that Jane's problem with him might be the embarrassing kind of problem that a woman has with a guy she's never gotten over. Jane always, even now, dressed unusually sexy when their mothers herded both families together. For instance, just last year at the college graduation party for Rachel, their youngest half sister, Jane had worn a low-cut sundress that barely covered her underwear, twice as much makeup as usual, and red stilettos, when usually she wore flats. And every few minutes Billie would catch her watching Ian out of the corner of her eye, watching to see if he was watching.

And he never was.

After ten years of that sort of uncharacteristic behavior, Billie knew Jane hadn't been able to move on. Billie *knew* Jane still loved him—or at least wanted him.

Who wouldn't? Billie wondered. He was hot. He had that tall dark god thing going on. If only he weren't an only child. A younger brother would've been perfect.

"It's been over a decade," Ian said now, lifting his bag to his shoulder. "We're adults, it's time to move on. She'll agree, I'm sure, especially when you point out I'll save her a lot of money."

Excellent point. Jane was notoriously careful about counting pennies. Becoming an accountant had surprised not a single soul who'd ever known her. In kindergarten, Jane had tallied up her classmate's milk money and tried to convince the class to invest for their futures instead of drinking it away. It was only one story among many to follow. Saving thousands of dollars with free labor would definitely take the sting out of seeing Ian Cooper now and then.

"If you're sure..."

Grinning, he walked to the door. "I'm always sure. I'll be back in an hour," he said. "What do you like in your burrito?"

"You're going to get me lunch, too?"

"Sounds like we've got a busy day ahead of us."

He was being too generous. She should at least pay for her lunch.

But she knew he'd refuse to let her. "Chicken," she said with a sigh. "Extra guac."

The memory of his grin lingered long after he'd left.

What trouble had she gotten into now?

Chapter 9

ON TUESDAY NIGHT after work, Billie drove up to her grandmother's—no, *her*—house and was surprised to see two enormous metal containers in her driveway. An open-topped, squat, green container for garbage, and a boxy white enclosed one for storage, as Ian had promised.

She just hadn't expected them to arrive so soon. After he'd helped her out all day Saturday and Sunday, she'd thought he'd be busy with his real job until at least the following weekend. Billie had started cleaning on Monday night after work, but there was only so much she could do with so much clutter in the house. The worst of the garbage was now bagged up and dumped with the rest of the stuff in the backyard. She'd been unable to find a square foot within the house to move anything. It was like one of those little plastic puzzles with squares that you had to move around into the proper order, except there was no empty square.

Yawning, she got out of the car with her takeout Thai and portable tea mug and braced herself for inhaling the smell inside the house again.

Then she glanced across the road and saw a familiar pickup. Ian's.

He was here again? Did the man never rest?

She sipped her cold tea. He was a gift from the heavens, and she was so, so grateful for his help, but...

She was tired. Sleeping on a makeshift camp bed in the kitchen had been a challenge. And then today she'd had a series of angry citizens to deal with in the permit center, and afterward she'd had her weekly volunteering stint at the library as a homework helper, where the ten-year-old boy in her charge told her she had nice boobs. And then expected her to thank him for the compliment.

So she had. Manners were important, right?

Yes, it had been a long day, and she'd been looking forward to curling up on her air mattress with her green curry and a beer as she scoped out home decorating pics on the internet. Doing imaginary work, not the real thing. But Ian wasn't imaginary.

She shook her kitty keychain to hear the meow before fitting the key in the lock and trying to open the door. It wouldn't turn. She tried again, but it didn't open until Ian pulled it open for her.

"Sorry, I changed the locks. That's why I'm here." He held up a set of keys. "I thought you'd want to be able to come in."

"You can do that? Just change the locks on somebody's house?" She took the new keys and tripped over the threshold. The carpeting was peeled back, exposing chunks of matted foamy material and shards of plywood.

"Careful." He took the Thai food and held her arm. "Great timing. I was starving."

Her spirits fell. But she had to share. Manners again. "Hope you like Thai," she said weakly.

He laughed. "Just kidding, Bill. I won't take your dinner. I ate hours ago. I brought us both a pizza, actually. Where've you been? I thought you'd be here around six or so. Don't city employees clock out right at five?"

"Hey, watch it. Public servants deserve your respect." She rescued her Thai and climbed over the roll of carpeting to get to the kitchen. "I volunteer on Tuesdays."

"I didn't know that. Where?"

"Library. Homework club. They need all the Spanish speakers they can get." She pointed at him. "I know what you're thinking. I wasn't exactly the best student myself, so how can I help?"

"I wasn't thinking that at all."

"Sure you weren't, Mr. Valedictorian," she said.

"Salutatorian. And I was thinking it was a nice thing of you to do. I should do something like it myself." He went over to the fridge. "I'll pour you a beer."

"Don't bother, just give me the bottle. I don't want to get a glass dirty. There's enough to clean as it is."

He got her a glass anyway and poured in the beer. "I'll wash it. It's better this way."

There was no arguing with him. Taking the glass, she looked down at the bare linoleum underfoot. "Hey, where's my bed?"

"Is that what you called it?"

"What'd you do with it?" she asked. "I'm not going to Jane's tonight. I'm sleeping here. I'm too tired to—"

"I've got a little surprise for you. Follow me." He led her out of the kitchen to the smallest bedroom—a room that previously had been filled with boxes, plastic bags, a treadmill, and several ancient televisions—and was now cleared away on one side, making room for a twin bed. A pink and yellow My Little Pony comforter and throw pillows were arranged on top like a department store display.

She handed him her beer, jogged forward, and flopped onto

the pastel-encrusted mattress. "Where'd you find this?" She laughed. "Oh my God! I used to sleep on this when I was little. In this room, whenever I slept over. Then one day she closed the door and told me I couldn't come in here anymore."

"I found the bed under the treadmill. The bedding was in a plastic crate with your name on it. The cats didn't seem to be allowed in here."

She hugged a pillow to her face. "It doesn't even smell."

"She'd double-bagged it."

"Ian, I owe you. This is amazing."

He was watching her, smiling, then abruptly turned away. "Well, I'd better go. I just wanted to give you the keys."

"You don't have to..." Although she'd been unhappy to see his pickup, now she wasn't eager to see him go. In fact, it made her decidedly more unhappy.

"I'll be back first thing Saturday morning," he said. "Eight. We've got a lot to do."

"Eight is great." She'd survive getting up that early again, probably.

"Great."

They went to the door, he handed her the glass again, and they lingered there for a few extra seconds before he was gone.

I should've thanked him more, she thought as she locked the door and turned the shiny new dead bolt.

Later, when she was curling up under her pastel comforter, she swore she'd make it up to him on Saturday. Somehow.

Chapter 10

HAVING ARRIVED IN front of the house almost fifteen minutes early, Ian parked his pickup across the street and waited, staring at the deceptively tidy front yard while he thought about the way Billie was in high school.

Growing up, he'd never really noticed her, primarily because she was a few years younger, and he'd seemed to have more in common with Jane. But then, one night, when he'd been making out with Jane on the Garcia's front step, Billie had waved at them through the window and flickered the porch light on and off, laughing.

He should've been annoyed, but it had made him laugh. He'd decided then that he liked her. And he still did.

Breaking up with Jane had meant not seeing Billie much over the next few years. He stayed at MIT, with summer internships in New York, and only came home for quick visits. From his mother, he heard about Billie's extended journey through community college. He heard about her classes in psychology and art because Sandra was worried they wouldn't lead to a lucrative career. But now, although she never had finished school, and working for a small city's building department wasn't making her millions, Billie seemed happy. Her boss sounded like a jerk, and she didn't like her job, but she insisted she didn't care. All in all, Billie was a happy person. Being happy was her default condition, and he admired—and envied—her emotional resilience.

And, of course, he'd always thought she was cute. Maybe more than cute.

He frowned at himself in the rearview mirror.

Don't go there.

Billie was absolutely, totally off limits. Dating Jane had done enough damage. Over the past ten years, with their mothers so close, family events had frequently forced him and Jane together. By unspoken agreement, they'd avoided each other as best they could, never fighting but never making small talk, either. Being quiet was typical for him, but not for her, and her sisters teased her about it.

Nobody, other than the two of them, knew why they'd broken up. He'd wondered once if Billie suspected, but a few tentative, off-base remarks over the past few years showed she had no idea.

Thank God for small favors.

Because Jane had always seemed more upset about the breakup than he had, everyone assumed it had been his fault. And they were right. But it had been unpleasant for him, too. In fact—and he'd rather stick metal splinters under his fingernails than admit it—he'd had recurring nightmares about their last moments together.

Therefore, every time he ran into Jane, he enthusiastically renewed his vow to stay far, far away from any woman who was already well-known to his family, friends, or colleagues. Because when things ended, and they always ended, he'd never be able to really, completely break free. As it did with Jane, events would keep bringing them together, often at the worst of times: holidays, weddings, birthdays. His family was the one place he could relax and be himself, not the hot-shit financial guy, just a guy. When Jane was around, it was less relaxing and he could be less himself. If he messed around with Billie, too... her *sister*... he'd never be able to go home again.

He could imagine what the sisters' family would say about him. They'd probably lock up the two younger half sisters, Holly and Rachel, whenever he came by. At the very least, it would become a running joke.

So then, why had he let himself become friends with Billie? He did wonder sometimes if it was worth putting up with the suspicious look his mother already inflicted on him whenever he and Billie drove up together.

But then he'd remember the day he told Billie that he'd quit his corporate job and given away his multi-thousand-dollar suits. And unlike everyone else, even his usually supportive mother, she immediately declared it was a great idea. In spite of all evidence to the contrary. It was long before he'd proven he could start his own firm, long before his own business was off the ground.

She'd sent him *flowers*. The cheapest, smallest ones the florist had probably had, and he didn't even like flowers, but he'd known that whatever they'd cost was more than she could afford. And there was a foil balloon that declared "CongraDulations, Graduate!" Which was exactly how he'd seen it; not an ending, but a beginning.

He'd appreciated the gesture more than he could say.

Which was nothing new; he wasn't good at expressing himself.

Except with actions. Hauling out clutter and updating an old bungalow—this was how he could show his gratitude for their friendship.

He continued to gaze at the house, remembering the weekend before when they'd torn the curtains off the wall. The fresh sunlight pouring in had highlighted the golden flecks in Billie's big, warm brown eyes. He'd forgotten to breathe for a second.

He rubbed his thighs. Maybe his motives weren't entirely about gratitude and friendship.

Maybe this was a bad idea.

A knock on the passenger-side window made him jump. Turning his head, he saw Lorna waving at him through the glass, saying something he couldn't hear.

He rolled the window down. "Morning," he said, noticing she had two guys with her, both young and strong-looking. He'd offered to pay for some muscle, and she'd found some that was going to suit everyone perfectly. "What did you say?"

"I asked if you were having second thoughts," she said.

"Second thoughts about what?"

She smirked. "Nothing."

"Just waiting for you to get here." He rolled up the window, got out, and walked around the back to greet the heavily inked guys in their early twenties. "I'm Ian."

"Shawn and Marco," Lorna said, waving at them but not specifying who was who. She had the same inconvenient habit when she brought people into his office.

"I'm Shawn." The guy adjusted his glasses, then held out his hand. Ian shook it, trying not to cry out in pain when he squeezed it. The man had a grip. That would be useful.

He'd have to remember not to shake his hand again.

"Marco," the other guy said. "But you don't need to be a

genius to figure that out."

Ian met Lorna's gaze for a second, guessing she'd exaggerated his qualities to them before bringing them over. Still smarting from Shawn's greeting, Ian only gave Marco a wave and a friendly nod. "Hi. Great. Glad you're here."

Lorna rolled her eyes. "Enough with the small talk. Which house is it?"

Ian handed everyone a bag from the back of his truck and led them across the street to Billie's front door. As he knocked, he unzipped one of the bags and pulled out gloves. "Everyone has to wear these. And a mask. It's good you're already wearing long sleeves. Keep them rolled down. Broken glass and cats are a bad combination. Don't want anyone losing an arm because they got an infection."

"Damn, Ian. How bad is this place?" Lorna asked.

"There's no precise way to answer that question," Ian said just as the door swung open to show Billie in her underwear. Or a guy's underwear—a pair of green-striped boxer shorts hugged her round thighs, and a white sleeveless undershirt strained to cover a chest it hadn't been designed to cover.

Ian began to sweat all over.

"Crap," Billie said, squinting at them. Messy curls covered one eye. "Is it morning already?"

Perhaps it was the chilly morning breeze, perhaps it was the sight of two tatted-up dudes leering at her, but Billie's nipples visibly hardened beneath the thin, stretchy undershirt.

Ian stopped breathing. Just like he had last week.

"Nice outfit," Lorna said.

Eyes widening, Billie crossed her arms over her chest and bent over slightly, as if the slight change in height was going to hide any part of her they hadn't already seen. All it did was give them a better view of her cleavage. "Sorry. Sleeping." She held up a finger. "One second." The door slammed in their faces.

"Keep it in your pants, boys," Lorna said. "Ian has dibs."

"Nice," said a low voice behind Ian.

"There are no dibs," Ian growled.

"Excellent," said the other guy.

Ian turned and leveled a hard stare at each one of them. "But you will definitely be keeping it in your pants anyway," he said.

They both threw up their hands, grinning as they nodded.

Ian turned his back on them to glare at the door, but all he could see was nipples. For the rest of his life he'd be remembering those nipples. When he was meeting with clients, crawling through traffic, getting his teeth cleaned, dying of old age—the nipples would be there.

"Dibs," Lorna mumbled.

He couldn't remember ever being so angry. He didn't usually get angry. But at that moment he wanted to break something. And then fix it and break it again. For everything he was doing for her, the least she could do was wake up and put on some clothes that covered her nipples. That was all he asked. She didn't even have to work. She could curl up with a gallon of tea and catch up on the latest news about Lady Di in her grandmother's vintage periodicals, and he wouldn't be the least bit angry.

But coming to the door half-naked?

Nipples. Damn it.

The door swung open a second time. "I am so, so sorry," Billie said. "Thank you so much for coming." Now in an oversized hoodie and dark jeans, she stepped back and gestured them inside. Lorna went in, then Shawn and Marco. Ian hung back, struggling to regain his calm. Just another few deep breaths and he'd be fine.

Billie was frowning at him. "What's the matter? Are you sick?"

Chapter 11

BILLIE DIDN'T EVEN recognize his anger. When had she ever seen him angry? Nobody did. He wasn't that type of guy.

He didn't even *have* emotions, according to some people.

He drew in another breath. "I'm fine." He thrust his bag at her. "I brought gloves."

"You're angry," Billie said wonderingly.

"If you don't wear the gloves, I'm leaving," he said. "It's for your own safety."

"Oh my God, Ian. I am so, so sorry." She reached into the bag, pulled out a glove, and shoved her hand into it. "I'll wear whatever you say."

Don't wear anything, he thought, which only made him angry again. Without meeting her eyes, he strode past her to join the others, who had gathered in the kitchen.

Billie was right on his heels. "Help yourself to the bagels. There's coffee in the pot and I've got every kind of tea you'd ever want, so just ask."

Lorna poured herself coffee and stuck a whole bagel in her mouth. "What do you want us to do first?" she asked, her voice distorted by the bagel.

Pouncing at the opportunity to clear his head, Ian slapped his hands on both men's shoulders. "These guys will help me clear the front room. I've got a plan."

And it didn't involve nipples.

...

Hours later, Billie found Ian in the living room, removing the last of the curtains with a crowbar. Bright midday sun blasted through the newly exposed panoramic windows like a supernova. Shawn and Marco had gone out for burgers, and Lorna had gone home with asthma. It was a good time for Billie to apologize to Ian again. She carried a glass of ice water with a slice of fresh lemon from the garden. She'd had to hack through the weeds in the side yard to reach the tree, tearing her jeans on an overgrown blackberry bramble, but it was worth it if it helped her clear the air with her old friend.

"Have you forgiven me yet?" she asked. He'd been hauling boxes and trash, and directing Marco and Shawn to do the same, for over four hours. She'd been trying to keep up, but she'd never been very athletic. She was definitely in the comfort-not-speed-or-brute-strength category. Thus the lemon. Slicing small citrus fruits was right up her alley.

"Nothing to forgive." Ian took the glass, lifted it in salute, then brought it to his lips. As he swallowed, the muscles of his throat flexed, his skin glistened, and Billie realized she hadn't brought nearly a big enough glass. Exhaling, he rubbed the cold glass against his forehead and moaned orgasmically.

That was a little too much for Billie, who looked down to escape the sight of his pleasure-face, only to notice the way his gray T-shirt was hitched up on his damp abdomen, exposing a trail of dark hair diving under the waistband of his red underwear.

Red? She may have leaned a little closer to make sure. She'd imagined white. Heather gray at the most. "I'll get you more," she said, forcing her eyes back up as she reached for the glass.

He held it against his chest. "No. I'm fine."

"You drained it in two seconds." She tried to pull it out of his fingers. "It's the least I can do. Let me make it up to you."

Because his grip was vice-like—shouldn't he be tired by now?—the glass stayed where it was. "You don't have to make anything up to me," he said.

"I overslept and embarrassed you." That was the explanation she'd settled on for why he'd seemed so annoyed that morning. God, she knew *she*'d been embarrassed (or was when she woke up enough) to realize that she'd answered the door in a flimsy tank and shorty shorts, headlights flashing, thunder thighs thundering, looking hungover or just laid. Which was totally unfair, since she'd been up past three cleaning and sorting, preparing for their arrival. Sure, she'd had a few drinks, but alcohol was a disinfectant. She needed all the germ fighters she could get.

He fished one of the lemon slices out of the glass and sucked on it for a moment. His oh-so-blue eyes stared at her over his hand. "You didn't embarrass me."

"Oh, come on. Shawn and Marco?" she asked, cringing as she remembered. "Their eyes nearly fell out of their heads. What kind of friend answers the door like that?"

He drew the lemon slice away from his lips, regarded it for a moment before sucking it one last time, then dropped it in the glass. His eyes returned to hers. "A girlfriend might."

She shivered involuntarily. If he were any other guy, she might've thought he was flirting. But Ian didn't do innuendo. He was too literal, too black and white. Just stating the facts. "Ah. Of course. Shawn and Marco probably would think we're more than friends since you're helping me with this huge monster project. Didn't you explain it to them?"

Not answering, Ian tipped the glass back and sipped the last drops of liquid. His black hair fell back from his forehead, showing off the strong line of his jaw. When he turned away, she heard ice crunching between his teeth. Then he walked out of the room.

Feeling suddenly overheated, Billie stepped out of the beam of sunlight and wiped sweat off her forehead, staring at the empty doorway where he'd exited. She took a cooling breath before following him.

He was in the kitchen, pouring himself another glass of water from the pitcher, looking out the window at the lemon tree.

"What am I missing?" she asked. "Please explain. You still seem annoyed with me. If you're realizing this is too much work, it's totally OK. I understand. You can go right now and all I have for you is my eternal gratitude."

He didn't turn around, forcing her to study the back of his head. His thick, dark hair was long enough to curl slightly behind his ears.

"That's all you have for me?" he asked.

"Is there something else you want?" She moved closer. "I'm happy to apologize again."

His shoulders visibly tensed. "Please, no more apologies."

Billie saw that he obviously felt ill-used, but why? She'd tried to talk him out of doing as much as he had. "I offered to pay Shawn and Marco, but they refused. Is that it? Do you think I'm taking advantage of them?"

"I've already struck a deal with Shawn and Marco. You don't have to do a thing."

Frustrated that he wouldn't let her make it up to him, whatever it was, Billie put her hands on his back and began massaging his tight shoulders. He was a good six inches taller, and she had to move closer and go up on her tiptoes to get a good angle. Under her fingers, he felt powerful but tense, as if coiled to spring.

"Please, Ian," she said softly.

Without warning, he spun around to face her. Not expecting the move, her arms remained raised, her hands now on his chest. Sucking in a breath in surprise, she began to step back. But he grabbed her wrists and pulled her closer. Their bodies came together, her soft thighs against his hard ones, her belly brushing the fly of his jeans.

"Please?" His eyes searched her face. He looked more unhappy than before. Furious, even. "'Please' what?"

Short of breath, heart pounding, she tried to shrug, but he held her too tightly. "I don't know," she whispered.

Chapter 12

SHAKING HIS HEAD, he loosened his grip on her wrists and glanced down, his anger seeming to fade. But he didn't release her. Rising and falling heavily with his breath, his chest moved under her forearms. They'd never been so close to one another. He wasn't the hugging type.

Not that this was a hug, exactly. She wasn't sure what it was. He'd seemed so angry. Was this what he did when he couldn't punch somebody? Just grab them?

She should've pulled away, apologized again, this time for massaging his back without permission. Slice a few lemons. Laugh it off. And then she'd tell him thank you for his time and talk to Jane about hiring a stranger to help them out.

But she couldn't move. She didn't want to, even though she *wanted* to want to. Of course she wanted to. But being close to Ian Cooper felt good, as good as being close to any man could feel—which was pretty damn great. He was tall and well built, and even his sweat smelled tasty.

When she realized he was staring at her mouth, her knees weakened, pushing him closer to her. When he began to lower his head, her lips parted involuntarily. She told herself it was only because she needed some air.

Slowly, so slowly, he moved closer. Mesmerized, she watched the flick of his tongue over his lips. Her own thoughts were scattered, unsteady, elusive.

And then he drew back, frowning, and let out his breath. Like a bubble bursting, the strange, nervous tension broke and disappeared. He patted the sides of her arms where he'd been holding her, roughly, like a quarterback with his defensive lineman, and rolled his eyes.

"I must be losing my mind," he said. "God, I'm so sorry. Did I hurt you?"

She did feel as if she'd been run over by a horse trailer, but she didn't think that's what he meant. "What's the matter with you?"

Her question came out more hostile than she'd intended, but he'd upset her.

"I—I—" He looked away, his scowl deepening. "I didn't realize how upset I was about—about—business. Last night. Lost a lot of money. Didn't expect it."

This was about *work*? She'd known him for a long time. He'd never seemed to let his business bother him before. It was always a game, always fun, or at least intellectually fulfilling. "Haven't you lost money before?"

He cleared his throat, not meeting her eyes. "Not this much."

Given his wealth and the years managing his legendary fund, she couldn't imagine how much that might be. She didn't even want to know.

All right, yes. Yes she did.

"How much?" she asked.

Turning away, he gripped the kitchen counter and hung his head. After a moment, he said, "A lot."

"Like, millions?"

He glanced at her over his shoulder, a flicker of amusement in his eyes. Then he sobered. He gave a quick nod.

So all of his behavior today had nothing to do with her?

Could she believe that?

"Why'd you seem so angry at *me*?" And that other thing, she added silently.

"I—I—" He stood up straight and looked her in the eye. "It was wrong of me. I apologize. I suppose I think of you like... family. My mother always said I took everything out on her whenever I got home from school."

Now he was comparing her to his mother?

Whatever sexy feelings had been coursing through her veins a few minutes ago were now as desiccated as the hallway carpeting. Had Ian Cooper reached out to her for a hate fuck?

And had she almost agreed to it?

Billie went over to the counter and sought comfort from the cream cheese. Lifting the knife, which felt a little dangerous at the moment, she slathered a fist-sized glob of white heaven on a chunk of poppy seed bagel and shoved it in her mouth.

Would she never learn? She loved guys. She loved handsome guys. She loved having sex with handsome guys. It had gotten her into trouble in high school, in college, in her adult life—always. *Girls just wanna have fun.* God help her.

"I'll make it up to you," he said, giving her another robust thwack before striding out of the kitchen.

As she was rubbing the bruise on her arm—perhaps it was only emotional, but it stung all the same—she heard Marco and Shawn return to the house, and the exchange of bags of hamburgers among the men. When Shawn stuck his head in and asked her if she wanted a cheeseburger, she shook her head, pointing at her full mouth and waving her bagel.

While the men ate in the other room, she stood there and polished off the rest of the cream cheese, wondering how much money Ian would have to lose before he got angry enough to actually have sex with her.

Economic downturn had never sounded so hot.

And then, disgusted with herself, she went back to work.

...

The following Friday night, Ian closed his laptop, took off his earphones, and stared at the ceiling, his heated massage chair on the highest setting. It wasn't enough to unwind the tension wracking his body. The thought of returning to Billie's house in the morning was tying him in knots. His jaw ached from grinding his teeth. His hamstrings were stiff from running too many miles that morning—and every morning that week—in his efforts to clear his head. And if he didn't eat something—he'd worked through lunch and dinner without a break—he was going to pass out.

This wasn't like him. Easygoing Ian, that's what his mother called him. If losing millions wasn't enough to upset him—and it hadn't, in spite of what he'd said—then seeing Billie Garcia in her pajamas shouldn't spark a nervous breakdown.

Lorna's voice startled him out of his thoughts. "I thought you were different."

He spun around. She stood in the open doorway. "I don't remember hearing you knock," he said.

"I didn't." She came in and stood next to his recliner, holding a pizza box. The savory aroma made his stomach growl. "Do you realize what time it is?"

"Time for me to get a new admin, apparently." After he freed her from the pizza.

"Nah, you love me." Balancing the box on her opposite hip, Lorna reached down and lifted the controls to the recliner. "Damn, full throttle. You're a mess."

"It's been a stressful week."

She scowled. "Don't talk like that."

"Excuse me?"

"You're not supposed to get stressed out. That's not your thing."

"Well, I apologize for disappointing you," he said.

She threw the controls down. "You'll find an even better investor. You don't need that guy."

He stared at her, not comprehending.

"Isn't this about Oldroyd?" she asked.

"Isn't *what* about Oldroyd?" He got to his feet and gave her an imperious, warning stare. As he'd told Billie, he had lost big money, but he'd barely given it another thought.

Lorna waved at the chair, but uncertainty had crept into her eyes. "This with the chair and the music. You're freaking out."

"I sit in this chair every day."

"And read spreadsheets and websites and reports and email and watch the markets. Not stare at the ceiling, rocking out to dead guys." She held the box out to him. "Here. I got it for myself but changed my mind."

Trying not to smile at the way she hated to admit to any kindness, he took the box. "If I were forced to listen to *your* music, I'd rather die myself." He carried the pizza over to his desk and eagerly pulled out a slice.

"If not Oldroyd, then what?"

He took a huge bite. "Nothing."

"Gross. Don't talk with your mouth full."

Smiling, he took another. "You asked," he said, his voice distorted by the cheese, sausage, chewy crust, and chunks of fresh tomato. This was why he kept her around.

"What, you don't know how to time your chewing with speaking?" she asked. "I've met your mother. I'm sure she taught you better than that."

Her concern was nice. And the pizza was already raising his blood sugar, and he felt his tension easing a little.

When his mouth was empty, he said, "Thank you. I was hungry."

"You should go home. If you keep this up, you'll die of a heart attack before you're forty."

He turned away to hide his shock. Grabbing a bottle of water, he lifted it to his lips and reminded himself she didn't know what she'd said; she was just being Lorna.

His own father had suffered two heart attacks when Ian was in high school, and a third when Ian was a rising star at a huge firm in San Francisco. Only the third one, which had kept him in the ICU for weeks, had gotten through to his stubborn father about the importance of slowing down. McIntyre Construction wasn't going to fall apart without him, but his family just might.

The day his dad had come home from the hospital, Ian had put in his notice at the firm.

Recovering his composure, he reached for another slice of pizza. "If you're worried about my heart health, you probably shouldn't be bringing me my own extra-large pizzas."

"It wasn't all for you, but fine. Your gross table manners have totally ruined my appetite."

Mouth full again, he asked, "What do I owe you?" and

reached for his wallet.

"Thirty-five," she said. "You can round it up to forty to thank me for my troubles."

With a laugh, he gave her fifty. "Thanks, Lorna."

"Whatever." She walked out. A few moments later, he heard the front door of the office slam shut.

He wasn't the only idiot still in the office on a Friday night, so he set the pizza down on the conference table, told his team to eat up and go home, and went out into the cold night.

His office was in a business park in Emeryville, crowded next to Oakland and Berkeley on the shore of the bay, across from San Francisco. Lorna had begged him to move the office to a building with a view, but he didn't see the point if they were going to have shades over the windows, staring at screens all day.

And when he emerged from the office at the end of the day, it was usually dark anyway, like tonight. He walked two blocks, past a biotech firm, an Indian burrito joint, another tech company in a renovated Victorian, and then to his loft in a converted cannery.

But he didn't go inside.

He wouldn't be able to sleep, so why not get started working on the house tonight?

Chapter 13

IAN TOLD HIMSELF he could get started on the bathroom floor. He also told himself he had to confirm that the debris box had been emptied and the new storage unit delivered, although there was nothing he could do about it on a Friday night after business hours if they hadn't been.

He had to see her.

For hours after The Incident, as he'd named it, he'd worked his ass off with Shawn and Marco, and barely spared Billie a word or a glance until he'd left with the other guys at the end of the day, and even then he'd only grunted a farewell.

They hadn't spoken since. Avoiding her like this was only making things worse. And lying about the reason for his bad temper had made him angry with himself, although he didn't know what excuse would've been better. Losing a fortune was a catastrophe that would credibly infuriate most men. But he wasn't most men, and he was a little disappointed that she'd believed him so readily. Maybe she didn't know him at all.

Maybe she should.

He parked his truck in front of the house next door and stared at the lights glowing from Billie's windows. The shades were drawn, but he saw flickering shadows that suggested she was moving around inside the front room.

He had to clarify the situation, that's all. They were old friends, he'd behaved badly last week but was fine now, she could trust him to act normally from now on. As soon as the clutter was out of the house, he'd tackle something simple but satisfying, like bathroom fixtures, or painting. Maybe install new lighting everywhere. He was itching to dive in and get busy.

And getting itchier by the moment.

He glanced at the dash. Almost ten o'clock. Too late to show up unannounced.

Too bad. After checking his reflection in the rearview mirror —he wouldn't want to show up with tomato sauce on his face for anyone, it didn't mean anything—he grabbed his backpack and went up to her front door. There he paused, realizing his heart was thudding against his ribs. He'd forgotten to confirm the debris box had been emptied.

As the door swung open, he suddenly remembered that not only should he avoid unnecessary alone time with Billie, he didn't want to see Jane, either. He should've called—

"Hey, everything all right?" Billie wore a brown, fluffy robe that made her look like an Ewok. The fleece covered every inch of skin below her chin, and even her feet were cocooned in padded sheepskin boots.

"Did the furnace break?" he asked. "You look like you're about to go dogsledding."

Eyebrow rising, she stepped aside and ushered him in. "I didn't have time to put on an evening gown. I know you don't like me answering the door in my pajamas." She closed the door and dead bolted it. "I was just going to bed so I'd be raring to go in the morning when you got here."

He'd done it again, insulting her on her own doorstep. Since when couldn't he control the words coming out of his own mouth? "Sorry. I didn't mean to sound critical. You look cute."

Jesus. He'd done it again. The filter between his thoughts and his words was broken.

She did look cute, and not like an imaginary forest-dwelling alien. Pink-cheeked, tousle-haired, curvy, feminine.

"What the hell's the matter with you lately?" she asked, scowling. "I don't buy the losing-a-fortune thing. I just don't. I wasn't going to say anything, but here you are and it's late and, no, the furnace isn't broken, I just learned my lesson from answering the door half-naked last week." Tightening the belt on her robe, she turned and padded into the front room, which was nearly empty except for a wooden kitchen chair and a single large box, on top of which rested a teacup and saucer.

"You've done a lot of work," he said, avoiding her question. Once again, he had to recover from a bad start.

She made a skeptical snort. "Not like you guys. And this room wasn't too bad. Grammy always kept it relatively clean for company."

He sniffed the air. "And it smells better. How'd you manage that?"

"I used chemicals known to the state of California to cause cancer and other horrible things."

"Don't worry," he said. "That warning's on everything."

"No, it's true. I've already started growing an eleventh toe. Pedicures are going to be a bitch from now on."

He grinned. "Where'd the couch go? And weren't there a few recliners or something?"

"I sold them on Craigslist," she said. "For a buck each."

"Wow. Great."

"Don't mock, big guy," she said. "I'm very proud of myself."

"I wasn't kidding. You scored. I thought we'd have to trash them."

"So did I, but then I realized they had slipcovers on them, and plastic underneath the slipcovers—like the wrappers they come in when they're new—and after I'd peeled that all off, they were in pretty good shape."

"Not enough to tempt you to keep them, though."

"No." She crossed her arms over her chest. "Look, if you're here to tell me you won't be coming tomorrow, I understand. It's too much. You've done more than—"

"You can't get rid of me that easily." He went into the darkened room and picked up her teacup. It was smaller than her usual mug, fragile and old-fashioned. The gold rim had chipped, and he considered warning her about cutting her lip. Or he could buy her a new set, something from England maybe. He'd like to see her face when she opened the shipping box.

He rotated the cup in his hands, dragging his fingertip over the chipped porcelain.

What was he doing here?

Trying to ignore the blood rushing in his ears, he lifted the saucer as well and began walking to the kitchen. "I wanted to make sure the new debris box was ready for me and the guys."

She followed him. "The truck dropped it off yesterday."

"And the storage unit. We filled it up last weekend. It would be better to sort it out as we go, but you'll probably need your family to go over it with you."

"Jane doesn't want anything. She's not sentimental, and neither is my dad. But Aunt Trixie is excited about combing through everything. She wants us to put everything other than garbage in those storage pods. I kept a few boxes I knew were valuable—photos, letters, that sort of thing—in the house so they didn't get lost."

They entered the kitchen, which was looking much better. The old countertops were peeling at the edges, but the crocks and ancient appliances and books and papers and cat-food containers were gone.

He turned on the water and began washing the cup by hand, rubbing his thumb over the rim where her lips had been.

Now, finally, he knew why he'd come. Lacking self-awareness had its advantages. If he were the type of guy who was in touch with his feelings, he would've known that dropping by tonight was too dangerous. He would've known that being alone with her in a house in the dark just might make him forget all those awkward family events with her sister. Just like Lorna warning him about heart attacks had made him remember his father, and how important it was to seize the day.

Gently, he placed the cup on a clean white-and-blue check towel spread out next to the sink. "You've really been busy. Did you do all this after work?" He spoke carefully, casually.

"I took another day off."

"Bet your boss loved that," he said.

She made a face. "He did not."

"Sorry," he said.

"Not your fault."

They stared at each other.

"I came by to explain what happened last weekend," he heard himself say.

"It wasn't a money thing, was it?"

"No."

She looked down at her hands. They were small and soft-looking. Her fingernails were all different colors. "It's something to do with me?"

"Yes."

One of her neighbors was playing very loud music. Or maybe it was that guy next door making kebabs out of her grandmother's cat. The screeching sound blended with the rattle of the old refrigerator.

He didn't say anything, didn't move. The robe should've been enough to help him shove aside sex thoughts, but it was having the opposite effect. The thought of unwrapping all that fuzzy fabric, revealing the sweet, naked skin beneath—

"I wish you'd tell me," she said. "We're friends, right?"

If he'd had any air in his lungs, he would've laughed. "Are we?"

She flinched as if he'd struck her.

Or grabbed her and pulled her close.

"I thought we were," she said softly.

"Maybe I want more than that." The words came to him through his ears, seconds after they were spoken, and he realized that he had been the one to say them, the one to send them out into the air between them, the one to own them.

Mouth falling open, she stared.

Those lips, those perfect little white teeth.

He stepped forward and slid his hand behind her neck, feeling the warm skin, the silky hair, the thrum of her pulse. "I've always wanted more than that. You must've guessed."

She gave a short, quick shake of her head that knocked a curl onto her forehead. Her eyes never left his. "Uh-uh," she breathed, her lips not moving.

Her neck was so warm, so soft. He wanted to stroke her cheek with his thumb but was afraid it would break the spell. Whatever was keeping her motionless, and therefore, he hoped, tempted, he didn't want to screw it up.

Was she tempted, or was he just fooling himself?

He needed to find out. Lying to himself again—*it's only research, like when you study a company's financials*—he stepped closer. Then he lifted his other hand and brushed the hair away from her temple, lowering his head a few inches, close enough to smell the lilac perfume she always wore. He gave her a split second to complain, to knee him in the nuts, to break away, but she was frozen and passive, waiting for him to do whatever it was he was going to do.

He was going to kiss her. Just like the afternoon years earlier when he'd quit his job, he was going to abandon his usual method of careful deliberation. In one hot, blazing second, he had decided to follow his instincts.

Sliding his fingers through her curls, he closed the distance between them.

Chapter 14

THIS WAS REALLY happening.

Billie felt his mouth come down on hers, felt his hands tangle in her hair, felt her pulse jump and fly through her veins like a sparrow—but she did nothing.

Inside, she was melting, burning, exploding. But outside—how could she respond to a dream? There had been moments, of course there had, when she'd allowed herself to imagine what it would feel like to strip off his T-shirt and cargo shorts and lick his pecs and taste the sweat beading on his throat...

I mean, who wouldn't? she thought, swaying on her weak knees as she concentrated on the feel of every millimeter of his lips—oh, and tongue, there was tongue—

But she couldn't do this. They couldn't. He couldn't.

He was.

No, no, it had gone far enough. They had to stop right now.

Right. Now.

Now.

Yeah, right.

He felt so good. She was so weak. Physically and morally. He was just too, too...

Perfect. It was as if a witch had cursed him with tall-dark-and-handsome potion. And then zapped him with the most powerful strong-and-silent-type spell known to magic.

Just a smidgen, she parted her lips. His appreciative growl made her open wider. She leaned into him.

Oh God, she shouldn't be doing this. This wasn't a potion, this wasn't a spell, this was lust. And her own stupid weakness.

One of his hands had slipped down her back and was moving slowly but determinedly to her ass. Oh, hello, there it was. His palm cupped her butt cheek, his fingers spreading wide and then squeezing.

Tilting her head, she sucked his tongue into her mouth, feeling herself get wet, reveling in the pressure of his hard-on and imagining it entering her right here against the counter, bam, bam, bam—

Holy shit on a stick, what was she doing? This was Ian. Ian Cooper.

Jane's boyfriend. Long ago and forever more, at least as far as she was concerned.

With more strength than it had taken her to free her Hyundai from a snowdrift in Tahoe last winter, Billie flattened her hands on his chest—his warm, broad, tantalizing chest—and shoved.

"What are you doing?" She pointed at him as she staggered backward.

"You know what I was doing." He was breathing heavily, his eyes as dark as her best denim jeans.

"We're friends!"

"I'm not convinced. And from the way you were just going at it, you're not either."

"Going at it?" She felt herself flush to the roots of her hair, the last part of her to reach combustion levels. "I'm a healthy female organism who's quick to respond sexually to stimulus."

A smile twisted his mouth. "Excuse me?"

Oh God. She'd just quoted that geeky male feminist studies grad student she'd dated a few years ago. She stood up taller. Better press on as best she could. "You heard me."

"You said I stimulate you. That's good."

With a bracing inhalation of Ian-free air, she straightened her shoulders. "I'm saying it's nothing personal, and we're not going to do it again." She tied another knot on her robe. "*You*'re not going to do it again."

"I think I just might," he said.

A shiver danced down her spine. "Even though I don't want you to? Are you crazy?"

He still had that damn smile on his face. "But you *do* want me to."

The tough, independent side of her wanted to pour the salad dressing on the counter over his head until he stopped smirking at her.

Part of what he said was true. But only part. With a few feet between them, and the urge to grab the Newman's Own Honey Mustard strong in her mind, she was able to shake off the lust and remember her vows, both to herself and to her sister.

"I don't, actually," she said softly. "I'm sorry, Ian, but I don't."

His smile finally fell. Eyes narrowing, he stared at her for a long moment. "You're afraid of Jane."

His exact words surprised her. Afraid, yes. But... "*Of?*" she repeated.

"Of what she'll say. Of being judged." He moved away and leaned back against the counter, resting one ankle over the other. "Just like in high school."

"I don't know what you're talking about."

"She's your big sister. You've always wanted her to be proud of you. You're still hoping she will be."

Her eyes darted to the honey mustard salad dressing, imagining how much better he'd look with it splashed all over his face. "That's a stupid thing to say."

"I'm just quoting you."

"I never said that."

His eyebrows shot up. "Oh yes, you certainly did. I have an excellent memory. You were wearing a green sweater at the time. And those big dangly frog earrings she gave you."

She hadn't worn those earrings since high school. A vague memory teased the basement of her mind. "They were newts," was all she could think to say at first. And then, "Jane gave them to me for my eighth grade graduation. She told me there was a lot of pressure to grow up too fast and she wanted me to remember how to be a kid, how to have fun. Jane has always been awesome."

"I agree," he said.

"Then—" *Then why'd you break her heart?* she'd almost asked. "You don't act like you think she's awesome."

"It didn't work out between us, but I admired her." He shrugged. "I always will. Which was what I was saying right before you said that about wanting her to be proud of you."

The memory came back in a rush. She'd been seventeen, a couple of years after the breakup, and he was home from college for Christmas. Curious to see him again, she'd jumped at the chance to go to his house with her mom.

While their mothers had wrapped presents and gossiped in the kitchen, Billie and Ian had played air hockey in the Coopers' rec room, having a great time, although she'd felt a little guilty about having so much fun with her sister's ex.

But only a little. It had been a difficult time to live in Jane's shadow. Billie had just failed physics for the first time, and algebra for the third, and was learning to accept she wouldn't be going on to Berkeley or Davis or Sonoma State like her best friends.

Unlike Billie, Jane had always been perfect. Not only had she been top of the class, but she'd never gotten a B, let alone an F. Her winning streak continued uninterrupted to this day.

Except with men. She still had trouble with that. Billie thought it had everything to do with the man who'd just kissed her.

"Well?" he asked now. "Is it coming back to you?"

The kettle whistled. She walked over to it, shooting him a glance over her shoulder. "Maybe a little."

That day at his house long ago, she'd thought maybe he could understand. Maybe he'd broken up with Jane because all her perfection had been annoying to him, too. Maybe he'd even been jealous, she'd thought. And so, in a moment of weakness, she'd knocked the puck to him across the table and shared her insecurities with him.

"I wasn't bullshitting you," he said now. "She really was proud of you."

She'd gobbled up every word he'd shared over the air hockey table. He'd listed her qualities—her people skills, her sense of humor, her generosity, her fluency in Spanish, which she'd learned to talk to her grandfather—that Jane had told him she'd admired in her. He'd gone on and on, telling her how much her big sister wished she could be a little more like *her*.

Jane was like that, often seeing the best in people and then emulating them so she could improve herself.

Unlike Billie. If Billie ever improved herself, it was an accident. She never set out to accomplish something for the sake of being amazing. Her vision didn't extend that far into the future. What she did, she did because she felt like it. She wasn't much better now than she'd been as a teenager.

"I was such a fuckup," Billie said, getting out a mug.

"You were not," he said. "You just weren't a good student. There's a difference."

It wasn't fair of him to get nice right at the moment she most needed to pour salad dressing on his head.

"Thanks," she said softly, keeping her back to him. She got out a second mug, this one for him.

He walked over and stood directly behind her, so close he brushed the bottom hem of her robe. "I wish I'd known earlier."

"Known what?"

"That you're attracted to me."

Her heart skipped. Hoping he couldn't see her hands shaking, she poured the boiling water into her mug. "I'm not. I told you. You caught me off guard. It's late, I'm tired, I responded."

"You forgot to put a tea bag in your mug," he said.

"You're too full of yourself," she replied, maneuvering out from behind him, her mug of hot water clutched in her fist. She saluted him with it. "I happen to love hot water. It's the ultimate decaf."

"You're nervous."

"Sure I am. You show up here late at night and make your moves and confuse me. That makes me nervous."

His smile returned, and with it a twinkle in his dark blue eyes. "Well, better late than never." His gaze fell to her robe, sliding over it from head to toe as if it were a transparent negligee, before he nodded and walked out of the room. "Get some sleep. I'll be back first thing in the morning."

She lifted her mug to her lips and inhaled the steam. Her heart was still pounding in her chest. She should insist he not come again, that the repairs were her problem and that she didn't want him around.

But then she heard the door slam.

Too late. He was gone.

Closing her eyes, she sipped the water, still too hot to drink but not as hot as Ian's lips had been.

She couldn't let this go any further. Jane might have a boyfriend, but the dude was the third guy she'd dated since high school who wasn't even likable. It was as if Jane were intentionally choosing men she'd never love or marry. As if she were still pining for her high school sweetheart, the only man she'd ever loved.

And who could ever top Ian Cooper?

Top... bottom... sordid images spun through her addled brain.

Billie hadn't been joking about being a female organism quick to respond to sexual stimulus. That's all this was about. Those broad shoulders, the high cheekbones, the dark hair curling just so around his ears, and those stunning ocean-blue eyes.

Jane wasn't the only one to make bad romantic choices. Billie's own track record was terrible, and her downfall always began with a kiss.

This time would be different.

It would be.

Chapter 15

THE NEXT MORNING, Ian pressed the doorbell, trying not to smile too broadly. He was more than ready to see her again.

He'd never been the type for regrets. Kissing her had been a bad idea, but he'd done it. And yes, there would be painful times ahead, littered with disappointed mothers and disgusted sisters, but he would work very, very hard to make those times as far in the future as possible.

He'd felt her respond to him. Those few hot moments last night had forever shattered the fragile illusion that they were friends. They couldn't stop now and pretend they could go back to the way they were. It was too late; they'd crossed the line. Since they'd have to pay the social price anyway, they should enjoy each other now as much as they could.

The lock clicked, and the door began to open. He knew better than to anticipate hot pants and nipples. She'd probably wear some daytime version of the Ewok robe to send him a message, one he'd ignore.

"Hi," she said, frowning so hard he could barely see her eyeballs.

He didn't try to hide his smile. Baggy jeans, a black fleece sweatshirt zipped up to her chin, bulky sheepskin boots. Her hair, every silky strand, was swept back into a tight ponytail and hidden under a baseball cap. She wore no makeup, no contact lenses. The frames perched on her nose were silver wire, not particularly flattering, more like an elderly man's reading glasses.

But her face was flushed a dusky rose.

She'd never been sexier. He took a moment to remember the taste of her lips.

Lifting her chin, she deepened her scowl. Her eyes completely disappeared. "What are you staring at?"

Marco and Shawn were still at the pickup, collecting the gear, so she had the opportunity to say rude things to him without being overheard. He kind of liked it. If she didn't care a little for him, she wouldn't get all riled up. She'd be more apologetic, gentle with his tender feelings. Fighting him was much better.

"Just happy to see you," he said pleasantly, stepping inside. "I thought we'd pull up the carpet today. You got rid of so much of the furniture, the boxes are mostly out of the way, the garbage out last week, and now we've got an empty debris box."

She glanced down at the floor, momentarily distracted. "Really?"

"We can't refinish the hardwoods until later, of course—there's lots more work to be done—but you won't have to breathe in as many fumes."

He could see that offer was too tempting for her to refuse. "That would be such an improvement. It's like walking on dead animals the way it is now."

"Go out for a few hours. The air is going to be unpleasant when we tear it up."

Seeing that he was only going to talk about the business of home repair, she visibly relaxed. "I can't just leave," she said. "That wouldn't be fair."

"Shawn and Marco work better as a team. You'd just get in the way."

"I may not be the most buff chick on the planet, but I can help. Somebody has to pull up all the nails and tacks."

"You can do that afterward." He waved to Shawn and Marco. "Front room, guys. Start at the corners. Cut into strips with the box cutters, roll it, carry it out."

"Please and thank you," Billie said to the men, then looked at Ian. "You forgot your manners."

"No problem," Shawn said, taking off his sunglasses, putting them in a case, then putting on a regular pair of glasses. He was very precise, very careful, which was one reason Ian thought he had a promising future. "He's giving us something way better."

Ian cringed, knowing she wasn't going to like the sound of that. He reconsidered Shawn's promising future.

Indeed, she'd perked right up. "How much?" she asked. "How much is he giving you? I need to know so we can pay him back."

Shawn and Marco burst out laughing. Shooting glances at Ian, they grabbed their gloves and bolted for the front room.

Billie spun on Ian. "How much?"

"Nothing."

"Oh, *really*."

"Not a dime," he said, grinning.

She crossed her arms over her chest. "If you think I'm going to suggest you're giving them sexual favors, you're going to be very disappointed."

He brushed his knuckles under her chin, quick to make any excuse to touch her. "You never disappoint me," he said quietly. "But it's flattering your thoughts went in that direction."

She batted his hand away and stepped back. "Cut that out. I know they're not doing this for nothing. It's my house. I deserve to know."

Maybe she did. Besides, he might as well tell her, or she would keep bringing it up. Last week she'd already offered the guys a few twenties as they were leaving. They'd told him about it on the ride over that morning, laughing as hard as they had just now.

"I'm giving them a little investment advice," he said. The twenties she'd offered them were an order of magnitude smaller than what the men hoped to rake in over the next few months. They looked like young bodybuilders, but they were actually smart, hungry traders about to make their first million.

"Only advice?" she asked.

"And the hookers and blow, of course."

She whacked him on the shoulder, but her lips looked as if they were fighting a smile. "Maybe I *should* leave. I'll need an alibi when the Feds raid the place."

Of course he didn't really want her going anywhere. "You can work in the side yard. I brought some loppers and hedge clippers. That lemon tree of yours could use a haircut. Clear a path to the back gate, and we can get back there to remove the garbage."

The sound of fabric tearing and plywood snapping reached them from the front room. She turned her head in that direction, indecision on her face, and then nodded. "That's a good idea, actually."

"Of course it is."

Sighing loudly, she bent over to the pile of tools Marco had carried in, found the clippers and shears, and began striding away. "Don't get cocky. This is still my house."

He watched her go, wondering if he'd played that right or

wrong. If he'd been too serious, she might've told him to get lost. Maybe if he joked about what he wanted to do with her, to her, on her, she'd ignore him until it was too late.

Until she forgot why she was pushing him away.

He grabbed a crowbar and sauntered over to the corner of ragged carpeting near the front door, a grin on his face.

Chapter 16

BILLIE WAS KNEE-deep in thorny lemon tree branches when she heard Jane's voice calling for her.

"I'm out in the side yard!" Billie shouted. About time Jane showed up to help. Just because she was contributing more money didn't mean she couldn't help clip the—

And then she remembered.

Ian was here.

F-word. And that's how she said it inside her head, too: *eff-word. Eff, eff, eff.*

She'd meant to tell Jane that Ian was helping out at the house. Hiding him completely would've been impossible, so she'd intended to warn her. But then she forgot, probably because of the mess of emotions swirling around in her brain. Precisely the type of brain that might make a person fail algebra three times in high school.

She wiggled around to the back of the tree, hoping to buy some time. A three-inch thorn tore a ragged line down her forearm, but she pressed on. Blood was better than emotional torture.

"Where are you?" Jane called.

For a moment, Billie thought about not answering. She bent

her knees a little to reduce her visible surface area.

"Are you stuck?" Jane asked, her voice getting closer.

It was no use. She'd have to face the firing squad. "Sorry, lots of thorns. Just a second." Billie tugged the sleeves down her arms, feeling the blood smear along the fabric, and pushed her way out again. A long branch caught on her sock, tripping her, and she fell to her hands and knees at her big sister's feet.

An appropriate posture, given the situation. For Jane to find Ian here was bad enough, but to find him without any warning that he *might* be here...

Billie stayed on the ground, digging her fingers into small clumps of earth as she cowered. Her sister wore black-and-white ballet flats with tiny silver bows on the toes. Knowing Jane, these were her work shoes. She probably wore them to exercise on the elliptical. Cleaned her bathroom in them.

"Are you hurt?" Jane asked.

Billie tried to decipher the tone in Jane's voice. Irritable? Furious? Disappointed? Heartbroken? She couldn't tell. Jane was hard to read, even for Billie, her closest sister.

"Just tired," Billie said with an exaggerated exhalation as she staggered to her feet. Playing for sympathy might help. Pretending to only just then notice her injured arm, she gasped and pulled back her sleeve, psyched to see the blood had smeared a two-by-ten-inch streak across her skin, making it look much worse than it actually was.

Little sisters had to use all the tools they had. Especially when their big sisters were perfect.

"Oh my God," Jane said. "What happened?"

"Must've been the thorns." Billie sighed again. "I've been out here for *hours*. There's just so *much* to *do*."

"Let's get you inside and clean that up." Jane turned and led the way to the kitchen, not bothering to pause and confirm that Billie was following. Inside, she went to the sink and ran the hot water.

"It's nothing," Billie said. "Just a scratch."

"God knows what germs are lurking around here. Here, put your arm under the water."

Billie did as instructed. It was scalding hot, and she cried out.

"Careful," Jane said. Her tone was unsympathetic.

Shooting her a suspicious glance, Billie turned down the temperature. As she soaped up her shallow wound, she chewed her lip, trying to think of a good introduction. "Did you meet Shawn and Marco?"

"Sure I did," Jane said. "My ex-boyfriend introduced us."

Billie turned off the water and closed her eyes.

"What a coincidence that he just happened to be driving by," Jane said flatly.

"What?"

"And then *happened* to see you in the yard so he stopped and you guys got talking and he just *happened* to have two beefy young men ready to carry heavy things." Jane handed her a paper towel. "Pat gently, don't rub."

"I asked him," Billie said. "Ian. I asked him to help."

"You don't say." The sarcasm was sharp enough to cut her arm clean off.

"Don't be like that."

"You should've told me," Jane said.

"I'm afraid of you. You're scary." Billie grabbed her sister's hand and put it over her heart. "Feel that? It's totally pounding. I'm still fighting the urge to run."

"Don't bother," Jane said, pulling free. "I'd catch you." And she always did, that was true. She was the marathon type. Anything with a finish line and a prize, Jane was all over it.

"He was just going to walk through the house with me once, give me his impressions, make a few educated guesses about repairs, that's it," Billie said.

"You really believed that would be enough for him?"

Billie's heart fell through her pelvis, down her leg, and crawled into her heel, desperate to reach the floor. Did Jane suspect he'd kissed her? That he'd wanted to?

"I don't know, why wouldn't it be?" Billie asked, her voice sounding funny to her own ears. "Who'd want to spend the next million weekends of their life helping clean out an old cat lady's house?"

"Ian Cooper. Come on, you know him. Remember when he retiled Mom's bathroom?"

Billie managed to take a complete breath. It was all right. Jane hadn't meant anything sexual.

"He was in college then," Billie said. "He probably needed the money. But now he's rich and I'm not paying him a penny."

"He's never been motivated by money. You must know that. He just loves getting his hands dirty."

Billie dabbed at the droplets of blood on her arm, afraid of the look she might have on her face. "I told him we didn't need him. I did. But he overpowered me."

Jane snorted. "I bet."

Feeling herself flush, Billie turned her back on her sister and began arranging her half-dozen tea canisters on the counter into a pyramid. If Jane was this angry about him hauling garbage and removing carpeting, how would she feel about that kiss? Or the way Billie hadn't stopped him?

"I'll send him home," Billie said, moving toward the door.

Chapter 17

"HOLD ON," JANE said. "He's here. The damage has already been done."

Oh God. Not nearly. "So you *do* want to let him get involved?"

"I'm not going to walk over there and make a scene when he's in the middle of something," Jane said. "You shouldn't have hidden things from me, but it would be stupid to barge in right now and send everyone home. What's he paying those guys, do you know?"

Billie was glad she finally had an answer for that. "Investment advice. He's their guru."

One eyebrow arched on Jane's smooth, round forehead. "They look more like MMA fighters than bankers." She lowered her voice to a throaty purr. "Especially the big one."

"Easy, cougar. I think they're still in college."

Jane dug a hand into the bag on the counter and withdrew a chunk of a sesame bagel. "You're right. Not my type. Andrew is the love of my life. I was just kidding." She nibbled few seeds off the bagel. "Not my type," she mumbled.

It was Billie's turn to snort. Andrew was about as charming as an earwig on an ice cream cone. If Jane was type A, Andrew was type Z—you'd have to circle back to the end of the alphabet to do his anal-retentive, pedantic personality justice. One of these days, hopefully soon, Jane would admit she didn't like him very much either.

Jane shoved the bagel into her mouth, shaking her head, and only then got out the knife and cream cheese. She smeared a dollop of cream cheese on her finger and licked it off.

"It has the same calories when you eat it separately," Billie said.

"Quiet. You're still in the doghouse."

"Speaking of which, at least she didn't have any of those. Dogs, I mean. It would raise the yuck to a whole new level."

Jane wrinkled her nose. "I wonder how long it'll take to get rid of that smell."

"It's much better than it was." Billie was disappointed Jane could still detect an odor. "Look on the bright side. Because Ian is here today with Shawn and Marco, the carpets will be gone. I couldn't have done it by myself."

Chewing, Jane pondered her feet in the cute ballet flats with the tiny silver bows. Her tone became apologetic. "It's not like I expected you to do all of this yourself. I was going to hire people to help."

"I thought you should save your money for the big things."

Jane looked up. "I have to admit it's why I didn't kick them out the second I got here." Smirking mischievously, she lowered her voice. "Especially after I met Marco."

"I can find out if he's single," Billie said. It would be great if she got interested in a new man, even if he was barely in his twenties.

"Of course not."

"He might be."

"I mean, of course you're not going to find out," Jane said, laughing. "Oh man. I wish I'd known what I was walking into this morning. I would've worn—" She cut herself off.

"A dress?" Billie asked.

"Shut up."

"I couldn't help but notice you tend to wear a dress whenever..."

"Whenever what?"

Billie was in enough trouble as it was, so she shrugged. "Whenever you're lonely."

"I wish I were lonely," Jane muttered. "But the damn man never leaves the house."

It was a running joke that Andrew had no friends or hobbies. "Why don't you break up with him? Please?"

Jane glanced toward the front of the house, where the sound of ripping carpet continued. "He's good for me."

Billie could tell she was thinking about Ian. How could any man compete with Ian? "You must know you can do better than Andrew."

Jane licked the cream cheese knife, sighing. "Can I?" she asked softly.

Seeing the nostalgic longing in her sister's eyes, Billie began chewing her thumbnail, hating herself. How could she have let Ian kiss her last night? She'd never be able to tell Jane about it without breaking her heart completely. Jane wanted to forget him, but even after what he'd done, she couldn't bear to be near him without longing for the past.

But what had he actually done that was so bad? Maybe if Billie knew *exactly* what that was, she'd be so horrified and angry, she'd have the willpower to push him away.

Stepping within arm's reach, Billie lowered her voice to a

whisper. "What happened?" she asked. "Back in high school. What did he do to you? You've never said, you never want to talk about—"

Jane turned around and began looking through the cupboards. "Do you have any good coffee around here?"

"Come on, Jane. Please? It might make you feel b—"

"And don't offer me tea. I don't care what country it came from or how much it cost, it isn't coffee," Jane said.

Billie sighed. Her sister was as stubborn as a two-year-old. She'd never talk about anything she didn't want to. "I made coffee earlier, but it's probably gone by now."

"Shame." Jane found a glass and went over to the water dispenser on the fridge. "So, I thought we'd make a budget. First we'll need to have an inspector over, see what big stuff has to be done."

"Ian thinks the roof is all right," Billie said, smoothing the bandage over her arm. Later, after a glass of wine or two, she'd try again to get Jane to open up. "He thinks anything on the outside is probably fine. As long as Grammy didn't have to let workmen into the house."

"I hope he's right," Jane said. "He so often is."

She sounded so depressed. Billie made a decision. "Tell you what. We let him finish up today, but then we tell him to get lost." She'd avoid trouble by avoiding him completely. Sometimes abstinence was the only practical approach.

"But you pointed out we need to save our money for the big things," Jane said.

"Once the debris box and storage unit are full, we'll thank all of them for their service and that'll be it," Billie said. "Then you and I can talk about what to do next."

"No, I think we should take advantage of Ian's expertise."

Had she really just thought her sister was logical? "But you were just getting upset about *me* doing that."

"Only because you didn't tell me," Jane said. "But now that he's here, we might as well exploit him and all of his talents."

Ian strode into the kitchen, a tool belt slung low on his hips. "That's just what I was telling Billie last night." He glanced at her over his shoulder as he wiped the sweat off his forehead. Muscles bulged, sweat glistened, hormones fumed. "Isn't that right?"

Chapter 18

AS HE WASHED his hands in the sink, Ian wondered what else the sisters had said about him. He'd overheard the last few lines of conversation, which told him they'd been arguing about him being there, and figured it was best if he faced the controversy personally.

"Like I told Billie," he began, turning around and shaking off his wet hands, "this is like a hobby for me. Exercise. A break from business."

"What's wrong with the gym?" Billie asked.

Jane touched her arm. "No, it's all right. I said it's all right."

"I'm just asking," Billie said.

He ripped off a paper towel from the roll and wiped his hands, then his face. He could feel bits of decaying carpeting, dust, and cat hair sticking to his skin. But the floors were now bare, and Shawn and Marco had just left for the day. "Working out at a gym is a waste of energy. If I'm going to lift heavy things, I'd rather those things needed to be lifted for some reason other than strengthening my muscles." To his amusement, he noticed Billie's gaze flicker down his body.

He propped his hands on his hips, watching her gaze take another journey over him.

"Maybe we should charge *you*," Jane said. "Like the health club would."

Billie jumped in with a fake laugh, trying to ease the tension. "We were just thinking you've done enough. More than enough. After today—"

"You know what? I think Ian and I need to go for a walk," Jane said, nodding her head at him. "We can catch up on old times. What do you say?"

"Excellent idea," he said, disposing of his paper towel on the way out to the hallway. It would be impossible to really talk to Jane when Billie was there. "Let's go."

Billie made some kind of noise in protest, but Jane was soon at his heels. They walked out the front door to the driveway, where the debris box and storage unit sat with their loads. *Better out than in*, he thought. The house had a long way to go, but getting the junk out and the floors stripped was a massive improvement.

Jane walked over to the green box and stood there, looking down at the rolls of shredded, decayed carpeting. "First of all, thank you for doing this today," she said. "Our dad begged Grammy to let him replace the carpeting, but she refused. He even offered to do it himself, without any strangers helping, but she'd clam up, stop answering the phone, lock the doors, avoid us for months. What could we do?"

"I don't know," he said.

She glanced at him. "Andrew thought we should've done it when she went to the doctor a few months ago. Abduct her for the day. Not ask, just do it. But we didn't want to upset her."

Ian thought Andrew sounded like an asshole. "Who's Andrew?"

"My boyfriend. I live with him."

He nodded. So far, this was the longest conversation he'd had with Jane in over ten years.

"I take it you're not seeing anyone?" she asked.

He glanced back at the house and thought he saw a flicker of movement at the window. "Let's walk. It's a lot nicer than staring at garbage," he said.

Jane looked over at the window. "Billie," she said, shaking her head. "Just like old times."

He didn't want to think about old times. He wanted to make new ones.

They headed up the street toward the huge regional park less than a block away. One of his favorite trails was in that park, winding up through redwoods to a ridge with a fantastic view of the entire Bay Area. The location was unbeatable. He lived down in Emeryville because it was an easy stroll to the office, but he figured he'd move up here eventually.

"Why did you assume I'm not seeing anyone?" he asked.

"No reason. Just asking."

"You said, 'I take it.' Why did you say that?"

"Oh, come on," she said.

Had Billie told her about the kiss yesterday? He took a few steps without speaking. "No. I'm not seeing anyone."

"Do you ever?"

"What do you mean, ever?" he asked. Was she suggesting he'd been celibate since they'd dated?

"I was wondering if you ever got serious," she said. "Or if you still sleep around like you did in college."

His steps faltered. "How do you know what I did in college?"

She shrugged. "You developed quite a reputation. Word gets around."

"Marquita Hansen told you." A classmate of theirs who'd gone to MIT with him. Unfortunately, he'd slept with her, as well as several other women in his freshman dorm. He'd had his own way of dealing with a breakup.

"Can you guess why I'm concerned?" she asked.

"Can you guess why I don't give a—" He stopped himself. He unclenched his teeth. "Why are you concerned, Jane?"

She took a deep breath as if she were about to jump off a high dive. "The last time I saw you, at your parents' Halloween barbecue last year, you kept staring at me."

Halloween? He thought back. "I was waiting to see if your shoes got stuck in the lawn," he said honestly. People didn't usually wear high heels like that up in Rohnert Park unless they were headed to the casino on Friday night.

To his surprise, she smiled. "I'd thought the party was going to be inside," she said, shaking her head. "Because of the rain."

"Dad had already marinated the beef," Ian said. "He would've fired up the grill in a hurricane."

"So you weren't—" She looked serious again. "OK. Fine. You were staring at me because of my shoes."

"I don't remember staring at you."

"Well, you were."

"If you insist," he said.

"And then when I saw you here at the house today, I thought... because you'd been looking at me that way last fall..." She trailed off with a shrug.

She was afraid he wanted to get back together? "Listen, Jane, I don't think about you," he said firmly. "I haven't for years, except when my mother or Billie mentions you or we see each other at a party or whatever."

"Great," she said flatly. She didn't seem comforted.

A horrifying thought struck him. What if... Feeling queasy, he lowered his voice. "I'm sorry if you *want* me to think about you. I didn't realize—"

"Oh, God." She held up her hands in a warding-off gesture. "No. Never. I wouldn't ever—you can't think—"

"I don't, I don't," he said quickly, relief flooding him. "You *hate* me."

"I don't hate you." She paused, inhaling another deep breath. "But I will if you hurt Billie."

Chapter 19

IAN COULD SEE the fierce protectiveness in Jane's eyes. "Ah," he said.

"When I first got here and saw you, I thought, well, what I said. That maybe you wanted to see me. But then, after I talked to Billie and you came into the kitchen…"

He waited.

"I saw the way you looked at her," she said. "And the way she looked at you."

Even her sister can see Billie wants me. He looked down at his boots, dusty and paint-splattered from other jobs, avoiding eye contact so she wouldn't read the triumph in his face. "And?"

"And I didn't like it."

"Not surprising," he said. "You don't like *me*."

"I care more about Billie than I can say. I'd do anything to protect her."

He looked up. "I care about her too."

"If you really did, you'd stay away from her."

He fought to keep his voice level. "You might have reasons to hate me," he said, "but Billie doesn't. We've been friends for years."

"Of all the women in the world, why her?" she demanded. "You could have anyone. You're rich and handsome and successful... Why Billie, for God's sake? It's always seemed to me like some weird revenge thing. You and I ended on pretty bad terms. So why get close to my sister? You two have nothing, nothing in common."

"Maybe I like that."

She shook her head. "I can't help but think how people have been telling me and Billie our entire lives how much we look alike," she said. "Once we were both teenagers, strangers would assume we were twins."

For a moment he could only stare. "Are you suggesting I like Billie because she reminds me of *you*?"

"I know how competitive you are. How much of a perfectionist," she said. "If you make a mistake, you like to go back and do it over. I think there's a lot you might do with your ego at stake."

He turned on his heel and began walking back to the house. "It isn't *my* ego that's a problem," he said roughly, even more angry than when Billie had shown up at the door half-naked.

"Just think about what I'm saying," she said, chasing after him. "You never were very reflective. You're not self-aware. Don't you think it's possible you want to relive the past? Not because it was so great, but because it wasn't?"

"You just can't believe this isn't about you," he said.

"Not me, exactly, but—"

"I'm not in love with you, Jane." He stopped and turned on her. "I wasn't even in love with you *then*."

Her face went completely blank. He saw something terrible flicker deep within her eyes. "I know," she said quietly. "As if I could ever forget."

His anger seeped out of him, leaving him numb. "I'm sorry. I shouldn't have said that."

"I would never talk about this if it weren't for Billie. But I'm willing to humiliate myself for her sake. I'm willing to have you remind me of how little you cared about me because maybe you'll realize that you're about to do it again."

"I'm not. I'm not the same man—I wasn't even a man then, for God's sake, I was seventeen. Seventeen, and barely. I wish you'd remember that."

"People don't change that much. You're still basically the same. You're ambitious and analytical and don't like to get too emotional about anything or anyone," Jane said. "You'll always put your work first. You can't help it. I know because I'm the same way. We're not like Billie. She's all heart. She's impulsive. She doesn't worry about what could go wrong."

He considered those qualities. "I like those things about her," he said.

"Liking isn't enough," Jane said. "She needs love. And I'm going to be the one picking up the pieces when you don't give her any."

He saw the tears shining in Jane's eyes and felt a mixture of guilt and rising panic. "Please don't cry." He reached up to adjust the glasses he didn't wear anymore. He'd had LASIK and never got used to it.

Scowling, she wiped her cheek with the back of her hand. "I'm not. It's the wind."

"I haven't had the chance to say it for a few years," he began. "I'm sorry—"

"Stop. Don't. Please." She turned and started walking toward the house. "For God's sake, let's not talk about that."

He strode after her, looking up at the house just as the door opened. Billie came out with the usual mug of tea in her hand, smiling at the sun, and waved at them.

Jane made a show of waving back, shot him a big, fake smile over her shoulder, and jogged up the steps. "The park is just up the street. I never realized how close it was."

"I know, isn't it great?" Billie's curious gaze darted to Ian. When her eyes dropped to his crotch, the desire blasting through him almost knocked him over.

He walked up the steps slowly, watching her watch him, wanting to pin her against the front door, tear off her sweatshirt, lick every curve.

"You forgot to take off your tool belt," Billie said, pointing not at his impressive genitals but his well-worn utility equipment.

"He knows it's a good look on him," Jane said.

Both sisters looked at him and laughed, cooling his jets as effectively as an icy shower.

Holding his head high, he walked past the sisters, still laughing on the front step, and went into the house for his gear. He needed to go home and clean up, think about what Jane had said, decide what to do next.

He was stumbling into a complicated situation here and needed to decide if it was worth it. Billie didn't want to get involved, her sister certainly didn't want them to, and their mothers' friendship would make avoiding each other in the future impossible, which is what they'd want to do if things got messy. And Jane was right—it would get messy.

He went back outside, holding his crowbar and second tool belt—yeah, he had more than one, let them mock—and strode past Billie and Jane, still laughing at him, down the steps to his truck on the street.

"I'll see you guys later," he said. Maybe he'd catch up on some paperwork tonight, or call his friend Ty and go out for a beer, or watch that game he'd missed. A little time to screw his head on straight.

Yeah, that's what he needed.

But just as he was dropping his gear into the back, he glanced up at Billie and saw the look on her face.

Disappointment.

And just like that, everything changed. Again.

She was disappointed he was leaving.

He paused and stared at her for a moment, feeling good just looking at her. Then he climbed behind the wheel.

It was too late to care what Jane thought.

Sensible or no, he wanted Billie. And he'd have her.

Chapter 20

AT WORK ON Monday, Billie's head was definitely not on the job.

He'd kissed her. He'd laughed off her declaration that he wouldn't do it again.

And then, the final straw, he hadn't. He'd driven away in his truck, never to be heard from again.

As much as she tried, she couldn't thank Jane for whatever she'd said to scare him away. She could only be annoyed with him for playing with her.

Obviously, he was all wrong for her. She needed a guy who was as mild-mannered and obliging as she was. They'd bend over backward trying to make each other happy, they'd never fight, they'd cuddle and snuggle together at home, safe from the pushy, aggressive world outside.

This was what she wanted, she told herself. Not a hard-muscled, testosterone-fueled, blue-eyed alpha male who'd always get his way because she could never stand up to him.

"Get out there, Billie. It's 8:31. You've already got a line waiting."

Billie bit back a sigh as she grabbed her tea and stood up. Her supervisor, a sixtysomething man who went by 'Doc' because he had a PhD in something unspecified, was glaring at her from his desk behind hers. He hated her guts, always had. It was the hardest part of her job. No matter what she did, how well she performed her duties or even how badly, he seemed to despise her.

"On my way," she said, walking out of their small office with its glass walls to the front counter, where she greeted the taxpaying public. Her real bosses. They despised her only slightly less than Doc did.

But at least they had a reason. She was the official representative of the office that issued city permits, or didn't issue them, and charged high fees and lots of red tape for the experience. With one glance at the line snaking out into the hallway, she could tell who was big business, who was small, who was a homeowner, who would be overjoyed that she could speak Spanish, who would roll their eyes when she did.

They all had their problems. Morning problems were different than afternoon ones, and huge development projects usually had more than tiny ones, but she never knew when it would be the sort of problem to keep her up at night, driving her to do yoga or drink chamomile tea at three in the morning.

"Hi, how can I help you?" she asked the first person, a woman with a narrow face and huge silver hoops in her ears. Her dyed-blond hair was braided into long pigtails that rested on her shoulders like frayed ropes. She looked familiar, but Billie couldn't place her. Perhaps she'd joined the parade of humanity that marched past her counter some other day and Billie just didn't remember her.

"I want to talk to Doc," the woman said, staring past her through the glass wall into their office. "I can see him in there."

"I'm so sorry," Billie said, "he's tied up with other business right now, can I—"

"He's eating a donut," the woman said.

Really? Billie was tempted to look back over her shoulder. Doc had been going through a Paleo phase and pressured everyone around him to do the same; if he was eating a donut, Billie wanted to see it for herself.

But she overcame the urge. "I'm sure I can help you with whatever—"

"I'm not leaving here until I talk to Doc." The woman propped her crossed arms on the counter and leaned closer. Her braids and earrings swung forward. "That son of a bitch owes me money."

Blissful relief flooded Billie from head to toe. It was *personal*. Excellent. He'd *have* to deal with it.

"Of course," Billie said, beaming at her. "What's your name? I'll tell him you're here."

"He'll know. Just tell him it's time to pay the piper. And he's the rat."

For a moment, Billie's joy wavered. The lady was probably crazy. She peeked at Doc, certain he would yell at her for interrupting his—yes, he really was eating a donut. Chocolate sprinkles, from the looks of it. Getting caught would make him even angrier.

"Excuse me, isn't there somebody else who can help you out here?" shouted a man from the middle of the line. "Last time I was here, I waited an hour and a half. I've got work to do."

Grumbling agreement rippled through the parade of citizens.

They always asked that. The answer was always no. Since the recession, the number of city employees had been gutted. More than half of the desks in the building were empty.

But maybe today she would make a show of asking her boss for help and they could see him wave her away. Then they could aim their fury at Doc, chowing down on his chocolate sprinkles on the other side of the glass door, and spare her their hate.

"I'll go see," she said with a tight smile. "Thanks for your patience, everyone."

They sighed like a summer breeze as she walked away.

Leaving the door open behind her, Billie went over to her boss's desk. "Could you come out to the counter, Doc?"

The donut had disappeared, but telltale chocolate sprinkles littered the goldenrod-yellow Boys and Girls Club flier on his desk. Brushing crumbs off his white beard, he glowered at her. "You should've gotten out there earlier. And if you weren't so slow, the line wouldn't get so long. You always waste too much time jabbering with everyone. This is city hall, not Starbucks."

"There's a woman here to see you," Billie said.

"What? Who?"

"She wouldn't give her name. But I think I've seen her before."

"Oh, for Christ's sake. You fell for that—" he began.

"Don't pretend you don't see me," the woman called out.

Doc went as pale as his mustache. And then shot to his feet. "I'll be out for the rest of the day."

"Don't bother running," the woman shouted. "I know all about the back door to this place."

Billie was enjoying this.

Doc braced his hands on the desk, his jaw muscle twitching. His eyes darted back and forth. Finally he sat back down and waved dismissively at her. "Stop staring and send her in. And don't expect me to help you with that line. You've got to find a way to be more efficient."

Billie went back out and ushered the woman through the foldout counter and in through the office doorway. Doc, who was standing at the door, slammed it when the woman was inside and began lowering all the blinds.

"So sorry about that," Billie told the man who was next, a general contractor she'd helped several times before. "How can I help you?"

Over the next three hours, she dove into the daily grind at a pace that she hoped wouldn't give her a migraine. The door behind her never opened, the blinds never lifted. When the lunch hour arrived, she'd just assisted the last citizen with a permit to run electricity to her garden shed, where she recorded a popular poetry podcast that Billie had never heard, but she assured the woman she certainly would do so as soon as she had a second.

She dimmed the lights, put up the hours sign, and stared at the closed door. Her packed lunch was in there. And her purse. If she didn't get something to eat and drink, she was going to pass out and cause a medical emergency that would end up on the Official Flores Verdes Twitter feed. Nobody wanted that, not even Doc.

She knocked on the door and pressed her ear to the glass. No sound. She knocked harder. Waited again. Finally, she cracked the door open and peeked inside.

And saw that which could not be unseen.

Chapter 21

WELL, THAT'S A surprise, she thought. She'd feared bloodshed and property damage, not *that.*

Belatedly squeezing her eyes shut, biting her lip to stop herself from laughing, she closed the door as quietly as she could.

But Doc had seen her. Their gazes had met as he'd looked over his naked shoulder. Above his naked back. And naked ass. His white, furry little ass covered with spots.

Billie knew one thing: if Doc owed *her* money, she'd want it in *cash.*

Now what should she do? This wasn't a good development. Someday she would appreciate the moment. But right now, she just wanted to rewind the last thirty seconds—it had felt like an eternity, like a slow-mo nightmare—and enjoy her state of blissful ignorance, even if she was dehydrated and starved.

Any minute now, Doc and his...friend...were going to exit the love nest and walk right past Billie. Should she wave? Give two thumbs up?

This situation wasn't in the Standard Operating Procedures handbook.

And just then, Billie remembered where she'd seen the woman before; she worked behind the counter of the sandwich shop down the street. Billie hadn't recognized her without the spatula of mayo in her hand. And the braids were usually tucked under one of the restaurant's distinctive yellow baseball caps.

Just as Billie had decided to make a run for it and hide in the courtyard until the afternoon counter hours resumed, the door flung open.

"You did not see that," Doc said.

Billie froze. He seemed to be alone now. Sandwich lady must've slipped out the back door.

"See what?" she asked, her nerves, like air bubbles in her chest, tempting her to giggle.

His face twisted, eyes bulging. She realized he was attempting to smile. "Exactly," he said, sounding like he was choking. "Good girl."

"I was just going to get my stuff." She pointed at the office. "Lunch. OK?"

"Why wouldn't it be OK? It's the lunch hour, isn't it?"

Apparently getting some wasn't nearly enough. He was still an asshole.

She slipped past him, grabbed her purse and lunch bag, and bolted for the exit, trying to act cool and casual about having just seen his flexing butt muscles. She'd never look at him the same way again.

As she found her seat under a tree in the courtyard next to her fellow civil servants, she wondered who she would tell about that day's adventure. Nobody at work, she decided immediately. That would get around and ruin his life. He might be vindictive and evil, but she wasn't. Karma was a bitch, but she wasn't. She was firm on that.

But she had to tell somebody. For some insane reason, the first person who came to mind was Ian. She wanted to tell Ian. Really, really wanted to. But why?

Because it was so funny, and he'd appreciate it. Jane would probably want her to report it as a sexual harassment issue and get Doc fired, vigilante justice for the man who'd tortured her for the past two years.

But that wouldn't be right. Doc should be fired for being an awful, abusive monster. Not because he's a human being who indulged in a moment of passion. Or some kind of love-hate quid pro quo. Billie wasn't sure what exactly had gone down—or if *he* had during those three long hours—but she didn't think that one mistake should ruin his life.

All the other mistakes, maybe. But that one, no.

As she bit into her peanut butter sandwich—the reliable budget choice—her phone trilled with a text message.

"Take the rest of the day off," it said. Instead of a photo, Doc's avatar was the lightning bolt logo for AC/DC, his favorite ancient rock band.

She chewed and stared at the screen. As much as she'd enjoy the free time, she didn't think it was a good idea to dodge the situation that confronted them. They'd just have to face it in the morning. If she went home now and had it hanging over her head, she wouldn't be able to sleep. And then, exhausted, she'd be less prepared to deal with this—and keep a straight face—than she was right now.

Instead of typing a reply, she turned off her phone and dropped it into her purse. Ignorance was bliss. After she'd eaten, at the usual time, Billie rose and reported back for duty.

Doc, behind the counter, scowled at her as she walked in. "I told you to take the rest of the day off."

"You did? When?"

"I texted you."

"Oh, sorry. My phone's dead." This time she stashed her things under the counter, just in case she got locked out again, and stood next to him, facing the hallway where the public would soon begin to congregate for their afternoon visits.

The scowl on his face deepened. She offered him a smile.

With his face as red as the pimples on his ass, Doc spun away, stalked into the inside office, and slammed the door, although this time he put the blinds up, not down.

Just then, people began arriving with their folders filled with photos and forms and wrinkled receipts, and she was soon caught up in the usual rhythm of her day.

Around four, wearing his jacket and bike helmet, Doc came out of the office, flung aside the counter cutout, dropped it behind him with a bang, and marched past the line until he was out of sight. He'd strapped the wrong pant leg for his bike ride home, she noticed. Guess he had a lot on his mind.

Apparently they weren't going to face the situation today. She hoped she had plenty of melatonin for tonight.

"Is there anyone else who can help you?" asked the lady who was next.

If only, she thought.

And once again, for no good reason, she thought of Ian.

Shaking her head, she offered apologies to the crowd as she reached out for the lady's paperwork.

...

Just before six, Ian was trying to decide what excuse he'd use to show up at Billie's house tonight. It was a Monday, not the weekend, and she wasn't expecting him. He didn't usually leave until seven, but he'd planned on making it a short night at the office—with the hope of making it a very long one with her.

When somebody knocked on the door, he shouted, "Save it for tomorrow!"

But the door opened, and Billie's face appeared. "Does that go for me, too?"

Chapter 22

TILTING HIS RECLINER forward, Ian pushed aside his laptop and got to his feet. "Billie." Her hair was up in a messy ponytail today, with uneven curls falling down around her cheeks, and her eyes were heavily made up, making them look enormous.

He almost strode over and pulled her into his arms, but forced himself to hold still. He didn't want to scare her away. Instead, he leaned against his desk, propped one ankle over the other, and greeted her with a long, appreciative gaze. "Nice to see you."

Her eyes widened for a moment, then she walked over and climbed into his recliner, kicking it back like a pro and closing her eyes. "I don't really know why I'm here. I just felt like telling you about work today. I should've called."

There was only so much you could do over the phone. "Tough day?"

She laughed. "Yeah." She shook her head. "No. Not exactly. Something hilarious happened."

"Sounds fun." Sometimes she shared stories about the crazy projects of the eccentric citizens of Flores Verdes, but they'd never merited a house call before. "Tell me about it."

"Hilarious isn't always fun." She lifted her head and began

feeling around the side of the seat. "How do you turn on the massage?"

He went over and handed her the controller.

"Ah, excellent," she said, jabbing at the buttons. "When I win the lottery, I'm getting one of these. Park it right in front of those big windows overlooking the bay."

He chewed his lip to stop himself from offering to have one delivered first thing in the morning. "Let me take you out for a drink. I'll drive you home afterward."

"Here's the thing, Ian. I can't. You might get the wrong idea."

"I'm well-known for having unusually excellent ideas."

"There's always a first time," she said, then flinched. "Forget I said that."

This was turning out to be fun. He went over to the minifridge and got her a bottled tea, the good kind that didn't have any stuff added to it. He'd made the mistake of offering her a Snapple once and would never do it again.

"At least have this," he said, handing it to her before leaning against the edge of his desk. "You came to talk, so talk."

"I wouldn't be here if I had anyone else I could talk to about this."

This boded well. "You don't have to tell Jane everything."

"Oh no. See? You do have the wrong idea. This isn't about us." She waved the bottle at him. "There isn't an us, other than being friends. Or can't we be friends anymore?"

"Anymore? Since when?"

"Oh, come on. You know."

He did know. And he certainly didn't want her to avoid him because of it. "Of course we're still friends." Closer every minute.

"I came by because I can't tell any of my other friends, friends other than you, Mr. Friend Guy, what happened to me at work today." She sipped her tea, drawing his attention to her full lips. He forced himself to look up into her eyes.

"Why can't you tell any of your other friends? Or Jane?"

"It might get back to him. I have another friend who works for the city. It's the sort of story that would get around." She rubbed the cold bottle across her forehead, leaving a streak of condensation. "Jeez Louise, I wish I'd knocked harder."

"Tell me what happened."

Sinking deeper into the chair, she played with the controller buttons. "I walked in on my boss. Right there in the office, having sex with a woman who came in and said he owed her money." She laughed, her eyes shining with amusement. "Can you believe that?"

"Doc had sex with somebody?"

"I know, right? What are the odds?" She turned off the massage and moved the chair into a full upright position. "They'd been in there for hours. I thought they'd left out the back or something."

Ian regretted it was unlikely she'd come over to imitate the scene she'd seen earlier. "What did he do?"

"He was standing up, doing her on the desk. One of the empty desks, thank God. Not mine."

He choked on his laughter. "I meant afterward. Did he see you?"

"Unfortunately. Bad luck all around. I saw him in all his glory, he saw me seeing him in all his glory."

"Was it glorious?"

"I'm not going to lie. He had surprisingly good muscle tone. I guess it's from all the cycling."

Irritated by the thought of Billie admiring her boss's ass, Ian pushed away from the desk and strode to the door. "Come on, we're getting that drink."

She climbed out of the chair and took a sip of her tea. "No, I should get home. I haven't had dinner—"

"You go home, then, and I'll bring takeout and some wine. You still like Vietnamese?"

"Sure, but—"

"It'll give me a chance to show you the spreadsheets I put together," he said, waving at her to follow.

"What spreadsheets?"

"Just a little data I put together about the house. A few estimated costs, a timeline, nothing serious."

She looked down at the bottle of tea in her hand, obviously trying to think of an excuse.

If he showed up, she'd let him in. "I'll meet you there in about forty-five minutes," he said, walking out of the office with his jacket, not giving her any chance to argue.

...

Billie had known she was asking for trouble, visiting Ian after work at his office like that. She'd managed to convince herself that she deserved a sympathetic, amused ear after the day she'd had. Bottling things up inside wasn't her strong suit. She was proud of herself for lasting as long as she had.

But dropping in on him in person?

Reckless. Now he was coming over to the house because he thought she wanted to sleep with him.

Which she did, but couldn't because of so many reasons. So, so many, although the only one she could think of at the moment was Jane. There had to be more. Oh, right. He was too assertive for her. Too confident.

She peeked out the front window, her sigh fogging up the glass.

The problem with assertive and confident was that it was so damn sexy. It was strong enough to hold up all her soft, weak, squishy bits. He could carry her away and gobble her right up.

She lifted a finger and drew a pair of sexy lips inside the fogged glass. As she was adding a tongue, a pickup pulled into the driveway. Moving so quickly she almost cracked the glass, she wiped away her drawing, her heart skipping.

She'd kept on her work clothes so that she could greet Ian at the door in uptight business casual and not slutty, comfy loungewear. "Hi," she said.

He strode inside with a bag in each arm. "I've brought food."

"Leave your shoes on," she told him. "The floor's kind of rough. Loose nails, splinters, that sort of thing."

He glanced down and kicked a staple. "You shouldn't be living here under these conditions."

"I know," she said. "These guys broke in and tore out all my carpeting. I should sue."

He smiled and walked past her to the kitchen, where he immediately began plating up the food. "How about you open the wine?" He tore off his jacket, revealing broad shoulders and a hint of skin below the hem of his T-shirt.

She turned her gaze to the bag and found the bottle inside, glad to have something to do to distract herself. Going to Ian's office had been a mistake. Interrupting Doc had been a mistake. Drinking this wine might be a mistake.

But, she discovered as she studied the label, it was a pinot noir from Petaluma, a vineyard near where they grew up.

Bottoms up.

"You said you have spreadsheets?" she asked after she'd uncorked it and set it on the counter to breathe. "You should know stuff like that isn't my strong point. I failed math, literally failed it, more than once."

"I know. It made you cry."

A funny feeling squeezed her heart. "You remember that?" She gave up being patient and poured herself a glass of the pinot.

"I felt bad for you."

"Felt sorry for me. Great."

"No, I felt bad. There's a difference. I would've helped, but—" Stopping himself, he held out a plate. "Is this enough spring rolls for you?"

"You would've helped, but what?"

He shoved one of the spring rolls into his mouth, shaking his head.

"Come on, what?" she asked.

But he carried their plates and bowls over to the old laminate table and sat, face blank, while he continued to chew. She'd known him long and well enough to know that he wasn't going to budge. Unlike her, he didn't feel the need to spill his guts. She'd make the worst spy, but he'd make a great one. Just like Jane. No wonder the two of them had found each other.

Giving up on the interrogation with that sour thought, she sat across from him at the table and dipped her spoon into the soup.

"I didn't want to make Jane jealous," he muttered.

She gaped at him, the spoon hanging off her lip and dripping onto the table.

He reached for a container and popped open the top. "Those last few months we were together, we argued a lot. She was afraid..." He averted his eyes. "Never mind. I can't say."

"You can't *not* say. Ian. Please. Not after that teaser."

Leaning back in his chair, he set his fork down. "She was afraid I didn't care about her enough."

Billie could see that hadn't been easy for him to say. As Jane's sister, it wasn't easy to hear. "Oh." What else could she say? That after the breakup, she'd overheard Jane crying to a friend over the phone that Ian had never wanted her the way he should have?

"I'll need that spare set of keys again," he said.

The sudden change of topic went over her head. "Excuse me?"

"There's stuff that will need to get done during the week while you're at work."

"But you're also at work. You can't miss work for this. Come on, Ian, that's going too far. Weekends are bad enough."

"I'm taking some time off. A vacation."

"But you can't do that for me," she said.

"It's not for you, it's for me. I'm not going to make the same mistakes my father did."

How could she argue with that? His dad had almost worked himself to death. "Why not fly to Aruba, or Patagonia, or Mars, or something?"

"You need an inspector to go through the house," he said. "They work business hours. Now that the junk is out, you need to get that done."

"We'll handle it."

"He's coming tomorrow at ten." He held out his hand. "I'll return them."

"When?"

"What are you afraid of?"

Myself. "Nothing." *Everything.*

She got up, went to the drawer next to the fridge, and pulled out the extra keys, deciding right then she wasn't going to fight his eagerness to fix up the house anymore.

She'd need all her energy for fighting the urge to crawl into his lap, slide her hand behind his neck and pull him into long, hot, deep kiss that would make it impossible to ever be his friend again.

Or had that moment already happened?

Billie dropped the keys next to the spring rolls. Handing them over directly might've led to skin-on-skin contact. She was just praising herself for her willpower when he looked up and held her gaze, giving her a slow, sleepy smile.

"Thanks," he said.

Knees buckling, she sat down and attacked her soup. "You're a good friend," she said. "So, so helpful."

"There are other things I could do for you," he said.

Chapter 23

BILLIE WAITED A second before looking up. His face was impassive. "Oh?" Her voice didn't even squeak. She could so do this.

"Plumbing, for instance," he said.

"Plumbing."

He nodded, slipping a forkful of shredded cabbage into his mouth.

She waited for him to elaborate. When he didn't, she asked, voice a little too high, "Is there something wrong with my pipes?"

His eyelids dropped down for a split second. "I'll have to look carefully." He lifted his wine glass and rested it against his lips, regarding her over the rim. "I'd be happy to do it."

The soup was too hot. Her sweater was too thick. She was going to ignite right there at the table and set the house on fire. The wine, which she poured down her throat to cool down, only made her burn hotter. She felt tiny flames licking her all over.

"Jane might want to get someone else for that," she said.

The corner of his mouth twitched. "I imagine she might."

Taking the moment to breathe, she adjusted the prawns into a circle on her plate.

"We don't have to tell her," he said in a low voice.

Billie could hear her heart pounding. With a trembling fork, she readjusted the prawns into a star pattern. "I would."

Finally he sipped his wine, set down the glass, and resumed eating. "I know you two are close."

"Very, very close." Nodding like a woodpecker, she reached for something, anything. Not wine, that was too dangerous—she moved her hand to the right—the saltshaker. That would do. She picked it up. It was shaped like a white cat. The salt crystals came out of the little holes in the top of the head, which wasn't very appetizing if you thought about it. Kitty brains? Dandruff?

"The food isn't salty enough for you?" he asked.

She shook faster. "I love salt. Can't get enough."

"Funny," he said, "you've never mentioned that before."

"Maybe we've never eaten together before."

His left eyebrow arched. "We've eaten together countless times over the years."

"Have we?" she asked, turning it in her palm to loosen the salt inside, then resumed shaking. "I'd forgotten."

"I'm pretty forgettable," he said.

"You know how it is with friends," she said. "Always so casual. You know."

"Casual."

"And forgettable," she repeated.

"Of course. I know." He reached over and wrapped his fingers around the shaker, imprisoning her hand in his. He regarded her from beneath heavily lidded blue eyes. "May I?" he asked quietly.

She dropped her voice to a whisper. "May you what?"

"Borrow the salt," he said, using his thumb to loosen her fingers.

She jerked her hand away, dropping the saltshaker on the

table. "It's all yours."

His eyes widened. "Is everything all right?"

"Of course everything's all right," she said.

He glanced down at her plate. "You're not eating."

"Now it's too salty," she said.

His grin spread from one side of his face to the other, then crept up his face to light up his eyes. He smiled at her, saying nothing.

"I guess I overdid it with the shaker," she said.

"I love that about you," he said.

Her throat closed up. She coughed. "Excuse me?"

"You don't hold back," he said. "It's a great quality in a person."

"A person." She didn't feel like a person. She felt like a bonfire.

He stood up, set his napkin on the table, and came around to stand inches away from her shoulder. She kept her eyes on her plate, destroying the shrimp star pattern with a shaky hand, waiting, wondering, wishing.

His hand wrapped around her upper arm and lifted her to her feet. "A woman," he said, turning her to face him.

"If you make any moves, I'm going to hate myself." She sighed and stared at his chest. The zipper pull on his pullover sweater was caught, jutting sideways, marring the perfect symmetry of the rest of him.

His grip loosened. "Why would you hate yourself? You should hate me."

"Because I'm in charge of me, not you. I should have more self-control." Every shred of it was taken up fighting the urge to readjust the zipper.

Inhaling through his nose, he dropped his hands. After a

pause, he stepped back, went to the cupboard, got another plate. Then he came over, took her salty prawns away, and set down the empty plate. "You should eat." After he'd set her old plate in the sink, he lifted one of the containers and put it in front of her. "I'll stop bothering you."

"It's not you. I'm just not very hungry."

"I'm going to go now." He pulled out his phone and looked at it. "I've lined up a few things later this week. Inspectors and contractors. You might see my truck out front when you get home."

"Don't you have a business to run?"

He returned the phone to his pocket and began moving to the door. "I've got people."

"I wish I had people. Sounds nice."

In the doorway, he stopped and turned. "You've got me."

Before she could swoon into the spring rolls, he was gone.

...

By the time Saturday rolled around again, Billie was thinking about moving to New Hampshire. She'd never been back East before, but the stories about voters in New Hampshire every few years always made it sound like a nice, friendly place with lots of trees and pancakes and flannel. The main attraction for her this week, however, was its great distance from where she was right now. And that she knew absolutely not a single soul there.

So unlike Oakland. Ian not only had been in the house on Monday, but also on Tuesday, Wednesday, Thursday, and Friday. Apparently, a financial kingpin really could take time out of the office. All kinds of inspectors came by. An electrician tested the wiring. A plumber installed water-saving devices that Grammy would've hated in all the faucets and showers. And somebody painted the master bathroom a beautifully soothing sage green, the same color as the paint chip she'd picked out and taped to the vanity mirror.

And that wasn't all. Although Ian never mentioned it, she found an estimate for double-paned windows on the kitchen counter, and when she called Ian that night to make sure he didn't give them permission to go ahead with it, he told her not to worry about it.

"Twenty thousand dollars is something to worry about," she'd said.

"It's not a bill," he'd replied. "Just an estimate."

"Which you haven't agreed to. Right?"

"You will not receive any bills for twenty thousand dollars," he'd said. "Think of this as the discovery phase."

That sounded like a politician talking, which is maybe why she'd started thinking about New Hampshire. Today, Saturday, he was going to tackle the master bathroom floor. The rest of the room was done, at least for now, and he was looking forward to installing the tile "like old times," alluding to her mother's bathroom back home.

Now Billie rolled over in her bed and groaned into the pillow, just thinking about facing him and his slow smile and power drill and tempting, seductive ways for weeks and possibly months ahead. If it weren't for that, she'd let herself enjoy the miracles he was performing on the house, *her* house, miracles she'd be unable to do or pay for herself.

Everything was especially exhausting because she'd had to run the permit center by herself all week since Doc had informed his boss that he'd be taking a short leave, not for a vacation, but for an unspecified illness.

But he was supposed to be back on Monday, so she had that to look forward to.

She pulled the second pillow over her head. Soon she was suffocating in cheap polyester fill.

No way around it: she had to get up. She should.

She didn't get up.

"We can work around you if you need more sleep," Ian said from above.

Chapter 24

AS IF ELECTROCUTED by the frayed cord on Grammy's favorite reading lamp (which was now headed to the landfill), Billie bolted upright, one of the pillows clutched to her chest, and gaped at the man standing next to her bed.

Under other circumstances, his raven locks and piercing blue eyes would be a guilty pleasure to behold. But right now—

She hurled the pillow at his pretty head. When he ducked and grabbed the pillow with minimal effort, her annoyance blossomed into a fiery rage. Leaping out of bed, she picked up a second pillow and hurled that one too. He was wide-eyed as it clipped him on the shoulder.

"I knocked," he said.

She thrust out her hand, palm up. "Keys. Now."

"But—" He began.

"Give. Me. The. Keys." She jabbed her empty hand at him like a fencer.

Brows drawing together, he pulled them out of his jeans pocket and dropped them into her palm. "I'll go. Let me know when's a good time for me to do the tile."

As he turned to leave, and Billie was recovering her breath, her sister appeared in the doorway with a steaming mug in her hand, which she set on the nightstand.

"I let him in," Jane said. "Here's your tea. Now apologize."

"No, that's all right," he said, waving his hand. "It's been a long week. Billie could use the day off." He left the bedroom.

"It's past ten," Jane told her softly. "He was out there waiting in his truck when I got here. When did you tell him to come by?"

"Nine," Billie mumbled. Great. Now she was the bad guy. She grasped at any excuse. "Why are *you* here?"

"I didn't think it was fair to leave you with all the work to do by yourself."

Billie set the keys next to the mug, which apparently was filled with her favorite tea, which her sister had brewed for her.

I suck. "Thank you."

"Please go ask him to stay," Jane said, then sighed. "I can't believe I'm saying that."

"He just surprised me, that's all. So did you. I was half-asleep."

"Just a tip. If a burglar breaks in, a pillow isn't going to cut it as far as home security measures are concerned."

I need to rekey the house again, Billie thought. *And I'll have the only set.*

She shoved her feet into her flip-flops and hurried over the torn-up floor out into the hallway, where Ian was lifting a box of tile.

"Wait," she said.

"I'll move these to the second bedroom so you aren't tripping over them all week."

"No, it's OK. I'm sorry I beat you up. Will you stay?"

He looked up at her, eyebrow lifting. "You beat me up?"

"Don't pretend you're not hurting."

Ducking his head, he laughed. "You have no idea," he

muttered.

"Will you stay?"

"Of course I'll stay, if you want me to." He lifted the box higher. "This is the tile Jane picked. Do you like it?"

A long row of compact square boxes lined the hallway. "You've already bought it and hauled it inside. I'm sure whatever she picked out is fine."

He set the box down at her feet and pulled back the cardboard flap. "It's your house too. Take a look."

The large squares inside were sandy-colored, flat, and extremely tile-like. Billie had never thought to look critically at tile before, so she wasn't sure what she was supposed to say. "Where'd it come from?"

"Home Depot."

"No, I mean—it's not Italian or something, is it? Was it really expensive?"

"Let's just say you won't be getting any windows anytime soon." He squatted down and lifted the box again. "Or food."

The expression on her face must've been bad, because he grinned. "Just kidding, Billie. It wasn't expensive."

His smile brought out a tiny dimple in his left cheek, a slight indentation below his cheekbone that was like the kiss of an angel. Or a flustered civil servant in her pajamas.

Oh no. She realized she was half-naked again. Crossing her arms over her chest, she turned and ran for her bedroom, mumbling another apology and vowing silently to wear a bra and snowmobile suit to bed from now on.

By the time she'd put on clothes and brushed her teeth, Ian was already at work in the bathroom, adding a nifty pair of plastic goggles to his handyman outfit. Jane stood in the bathtub, listening carefully to Ian's explanation of what he was doing, which seemed to involve lots of moving around on his hands and knees looking really hot.

Billie paused in the hallway, moving her gaze from Ian's strong thighs to her sister's face. It had softened, looking younger, more relaxed, as Ian talked about measuring twice and cutting once, and how he'd forgotten to do that years ago in their mother's bathroom and had spent more money on materials, correcting his mistakes, than he'd earned when it was over.

"You never told me that," Jane said, tossing her head back and laughing. Although it was more like a giggle than her usual throaty, cynical chortle. When she saw Billie, she sobered. "He's teaching me a few skills in case the accounting doesn't pan out."

"I'm the one who needs a few skills," Billie said, thinking of facing Doc on Monday. "I'll never get a promotion at work if I don't learn more about construction and building codes."

"Do you really see yourself having a future in building permits?" Jane asked.

Her sister knew her too well. As it turned out, Billie had no interest in learning more than she'd already been forced to learn. But she didn't want to admit that in front of Ian. "Absolutely. It's fascinating stuff."

"Stick around," Ian said. "I'll teach you everything I know."

"There isn't room in the bathtub," Billie said.

Jane quickly climbed out. "I'm not staying. I'm sure Ian will work better on his own."

Ian tilted back on his heels and looked up at Billie. "I don't mind a little help." His eyelashes were long and dark, framing those pools of blue so well she lost her train of thought.

"Billie and I are going to talk about painting," Jane said,

patting her arm as she walked out of the bathroom. A few seconds later, she called out from deep inside the house. "You coming?"

Billie hesitated, drawn to Ian like cat hair to butter.

"Sorry again about this morning," she said.

"Don't apologize. I shouldn't have gone into your bedroom."

"I shouldn't have overslept," she said. "I don't really wake up until eleven."

He got to his feet and looked into her eyes. A tiny, star-shaped scar interrupted his left eyebrow, she noticed. "Then I'll come later from now on."

As Billie felt a heat flare between her thighs, Jane's voice reached her. "Belinda Emily Garcia," she called out.

Billie turned. "I have to go."

"Wait," he said, touching her arm. "Are you sure you like the tile she picked out?"

The eyelashes distracted her again, pulling her into a tunnel where all she could see was his face and its gentle concern. He was always thoughtful. Even when he was high-handed, he was kind.

She nodded. Her heart was beating too fast. Her throat was dry.

"Jane has always had excellent taste," she said softly, holding his gaze.

When his expression changed, its kindness becoming predatory, she turned and made a run for it, joining her sister in the living room to talk about paint.

Chapter 25

AT THE END of the day, Ian finished sealing the grout on the new tile floor and squatted back on his heels, wiping the sweat off his brow. Billie and Jane had gone to the paint store again. While he'd tiled the floor, they'd washed the living room walls and masked the window frames, or begun doing so. He'd known better than to suggest he pay for a professional crew to come in and do it all in a day or two. Neither one of them would've agreed to that. But that was fine. He liked anything that kept Billie within eye range. And her voice was nice to listen to also, especially when it said certain things.

Jane has always had good taste.

He stood, brushing dust off his jeans, and checked the time. Just after six. If he ran home for a shower, he might miss the chance to have dinner with her. He'd overheard Jane mention plans with her boyfriend, so she'd be out of the way, and he wasn't going to let that opportunity pass him by.

He'd just have to take a shower here. Not in the master bath, which would need time for the tile to cure, but in the smaller one off the hall. Before that, though, he'd order something from one of her favorite restaurants and have it delivered.

Soon he was showering inside the canary-yellow bathtub,

sudsing up his hair with cheap apple-scented shampoo. The bottle was mostly empty, diluted with water to extend the last ounce, and he regretted having to use it. She obviously pinched every penny. If she'd let him—

First things first.

The water pressure was pretty good, considering the flow-reducing emitters the plumber had put in, especially after he turned the head to its massage setting. He'd always been a sucker for massage and remembered the look on Billie's face when she'd rested in his recliner at work. He'd never tell her, but her new shower nozzle had cost more than all of the tile materials put together.

When he stepped out of the tub, dripping onto the bare peach-and-lime vinyl floor, he realized his mistake.

No towel. They'd cleaned out the cabinets, deciding to recycle everything after a few sniffs detected cat, cat, and more cat. There wasn't a piece of fabric in the room except for his own dirty clothes. The toilet paper was tempting, but it was the cheap kind that shredded in your hand, not the fluffy kind advertised on TV with cartoon bears.

After shaking his arms and wiping off his legs, he went over to the door and peeked out. It seemed quiet. "Billie?"

No answer. He glanced back at his dirty clothes. He'd have to put them back on anyway, but he'd rather dry off first. The hallway was empty. His bag with a few clean shop towels was only about ten feet away, resting on top of the leftover boxes of tile by the door.

He reached it in three strides, grabbing the bag's strap with one hand as his bare heel struck an exposed staple. Flinching from the pain, he pivoted on his good foot, hopped back to the bathroom, and shut the door behind him, heart pounding harder than it did at the end of a five-mile run.

If she'd seen him walking around naked, she would've kicked him out for sure. During their meal on Monday, he'd decided not to do anything until she was ready for it. One stolen kiss or a single night of forbidden fun wouldn't be enough for him. This morning's pillow assault had reminded him she didn't like him making himself too much at home. This was her house, and he'd have to be more careful about respecting her privacy.

Exhaling, he found a small white towel, fluffy and new, and patted his skin dry. His heel had survived serious damage, as had his pride, and by the time he stepped out of the bathroom in his jeans and T-shirt, he was feeling pretty good. He went to the kitchen to mix a drink for Billie to have when she returned.

But she was already there, sitting at the breakfast table with a stack of paint samples in her hand. And she had a drink.

He paused in the doorway. "I didn't realize you'd gotten back."

Murmuring something he couldn't hear, she lifted her glass and took a sip as she continued to flip through the paint samples.

"I hope it's all right I took a shower." To his surprise, he found himself lying. "I got some grout dust in my eyes. Had to wash it out right away."

She nodded, still looking at the colors, and took another drink. "Jane went home."

His hair, still damp, fell into his eyes. He wiped the droplets off his forehead. "I ordered Indian food," he said. "It should be here any minute."

"Sounds good." She stared down into her glass, tilting it back and forth.

Her remoteness was making him uncomfortable. Wanting a reaction, he lifted his bare foot and studied the heel that had been punctured by the staple. "Do you have a first aid kit? I stepped on something."

Finally she looked at him, appearing alarmed at first, but then skeptical. "Don't you have your own kit in the hall? You told everyone it was there if they needed it."

Smart woman. But he wouldn't give up that easily. "I don't have a bandage that's the right size."

Too sweet to suspect him of lying so blatantly, she got to her feet and went over to a drawer. "I have a box, but they're the cheap ones. They don't stick very well." She turned, holding it out to him, eyes slightly averted, not moving any closer.

He walked over and grasped the box, letting his fingers settle over hers and then leaving them there, curious to see what she would do. Her skin was soft but cold, and as the seconds ticked by, her tension increased until he could almost hear the air thrumming with it.

He edged closer, turning his wrist so he was clasping her hand, not the box, and when she sucked in a breath but didn't move, he slid his hand higher, stroking the tender skin of her wrist with his thumb.

That morning, when she'd said her sister had good taste, he'd nearly chased her down the hall and kissed her again, not caring that Jane was there.

Jane wasn't there now.

"Ian," she said, closing her eyes.

This time he wouldn't let her get away. "Billie," he said, capturing her face in both hands and crushing his mouth against hers.

Chapter 26

OH, BILLIE THOUGHT.

It wasn't really so much a thought as a breath. A sigh. His mouth was hard and soft and fast and slow, making her want to spend a lifetime tasting it. Hours and days and weeks of craving coalesced into a single moment, this lifetime in a kiss. Him. Here. This was what she wanted; he was what she wanted. But she shouldn't—

He slanted his head over hers and drove his tongue into her mouth.

Yes. Oh God. Yes, she should.

Billie lifted her hands to his shoulders and opened her mouth wider, arching against his body, inhaling all his scents—shampoo and sweat, soap and dust, Ian and Cooper.

"I'm so weak," she whispered, kissing the corner of his mouth, the curve of his chin, the dimple. "I knew this was going to happen."

"Billie." His arms came around her, drawing her closer.

The sound of her name on his lips sent tendrils of fire down her spine. Was this really happening? She tunneled her fingers into his hair, glorying in the silky feel of the thick strands, pulling his head closer to hers. His stubble was rough against her chin, which she loved. She rubbed against him like a cat until he caught her face again and forced her to concentrate on kissing.

Their tongues met in her mouth, then in his. The rest of the world fell away as she began to vibrate under his deft touch.

If she'd been able to hold a coherent thought, that thought would be: *he's really good at this.*

But at the moment, all she could do was invite him in and cling to him and stay on her feet where she could get more.

She'd changed into a loose scoop-necked top before she'd gone with Jane to the paint store, one of her favorites, and under that was her good-luck bra, a pink, lacy garment that didn't look like the sort of thing she would wear but always made her feel sexy.

Although not in the same galaxy of sexy as how Ian was making her feel when he broke away from her mouth to kiss his way down her neck. His whiskers raked across her delicate skin, sending tantalizing shockwaves to her core. She clung to him and let her head fall back, inviting him to do whatever he wanted as soon as possible.

The world faded away, leaving only the sensation of his rough fingers dragging across her belly, up her ribs, her arms—

He was lifting her shirt. It was lifted, it was over her head, it was flying through the air.

It was gone. She stood there in her bra and tightest jeans, too dazed to remember to suck in her stomach.

"Jesus," he said, looking her over slowly, taking in every inch from her head to her toes, with a lot of delays in between. Finally his gaze rested on the pink lace and the erect nipples trapped beneath it.

The desire in his eyes undid her. She reached for him, unwilling to wait another moment, shoving her hands under his shirt and flattening them against hard, soft skin and then exploring the contours of his stomach, up to his chest, where she delighted in the thick hair she'd imagined.

"Promise me you won't regret this," he said roughly.

She grabbed the hem of his shirt and lifted it up so she could taste him, lick him, smell him. Everywhere.

Breathing heavily, he caught her hands. His shirt fell back down. "Say it."

"Say what?"

"Say, 'I'm not going to regret this,'" he said. "'I'm not going to hate myself.'"

"You should never hate yourself." She wanted to nibble on him but he was holding her too tightly.

"Billie."

She gathered her wits. Would she hate herself? All week she'd thought about moving away instead of facing him and her family. But maybe that was the wrong approach. Maybe she had to live her own life and let other people live theirs.

This was her chance to be with a man who was worth something. Not money. The other stuff. All right, not *that* other stuff. The really important things, like character, intelligence, humor...

"Billie, please," he asked tightly.

"I'm not going to regret this," she said, knowing it was true. Whatever the cost, she'd pay it.

He pulled her against him like he had that day when he'd been angry and she hadn't known why. They stared into each other's eyes, chests rising and falling with their hurried breaths, saying nothing, saying everything.

Then he broke away, one hand still in his grasp, and pulled her with him out of the kitchen to the room where she slept, to the only bed in the house. There he paused, holding her at arm's length for a moment before ducking his head and biting her shoulder. No, the bra strap. He'd caught it between his teeth and was dragging it down the curve of her arm, his whiskers and his breath leaving a trail of molten honey as he pulled. When he reached the crook of her elbow, his mouth opened, releasing the strap, and then he moved to the other shoulder, trailing kisses along her collarbone. His teeth dragged the other strap down. There he began kissing her skin in the tender corner, slowly, nibbling with his lips and licking her like a kitten with a bowl of cream.

Unsteady on her feet, she watched the top of his dark head as he made love to her arm, vaguely aware she'd never been so turned on in her life, which was saying something. Until now, sex had been a quicker, more hurried business. She wasn't blaming any of her partners, either. God knows she was impatient and had no self-control, and wasn't that exactly why she was standing here right now with Ian Cooper giving her love bites next to the little infinity tattoo she'd had since she was nineteen?

Oh, it tickled. Laughing, she pulled her arm free and tackled every inch of his six-foot-one frame to the bed. He grunted as she landed on top of him, then somehow flipped her onto her back before she could take off his shirt, which had been her primary objective.

"I was in the middle of something," he growled, pinning her on the bed by the shoulders. His gaze fell to her chest. "This."

Giving up on removing his shirt for the moment, she went limp as he ducked his head again and bit down on the lacy cup of her bra.

And her nipple beneath it.

It didn't hurt, except in the way that unfulfilled sexual arousal hurt, which was probably why she cried out and began bucking on the bed beneath him as he nibbled and sucked. His hands remained on her shoulders, gently holding her in place.

When he turned his attention to the other nipple, she let out another cry and grabbed fistfuls of the quilt beneath her. Vaguely she thought it would've been better if they'd removed it first, since it was a pain to fit it in the washing machine, but then his hands were sliding around her ribs to the clasp of her bra and it was falling away, flying away, and he was there again and there was nothing between his mouth and her skin, nothing at all.

Fed up with the delay, she released the quilt and grabbed the hem of his T-shirt and finally, heedless of her nails raking across his skin, lifted the shirt up to his chin. He leaned back and lifted his arms to free it completely, giving her a breathtaking view of his muscles flexing over his broad chest and arms, those triceps and pecs and whatever else they were called. She didn't care; they were all beautiful. He was beautiful.

Suddenly terrified, she lowered her hands to the quilt again and held on for dear life. He straddled her, gazing into her eyes. For several long heartbeats, neither of them moved.

She was topless, and he was topless, but they both wore jeans. This thought seemed to strike both of them at the same time, because they simultaneously reached for their waistbands—he to hers, she to his. The confirmation that great minds really did think alike made both of them laugh, and the fear that had gripped Billie a second earlier vanished.

His dark hair trailed down his abdomen into a pair of sapphire-blue boxer briefs that later she'd ask if he'd chosen because they brought out his pretty eyes. Later. Now she wasn't thinking about making jokes, only about the way his skin got softer just beneath the elastic band and how he groaned as her hand journeyed all the way down.

He broke away and removed the jeans and boxers as fast as she'd ever seen the maneuver accomplished, giving her a too-quick view of his muscled thighs and ass.

Like the view she'd had about thirty minutes earlier when he'd run out to get that little towel.

She'd tell him about that later.

The other part of him looked different than it had earlier. Bigger and better, in fact.

She was going to touch him and kiss him and have him inside her. Ian. Ian Cooper. They were going to do things and go places she'd sworn they wouldn't. Because she was so, so bad, this turned her on more than she'd ever been in her life.

I shouldn't. I shouldn't do this. I have to do this. This is all I've ever wanted. Yes, yes, yes.

His gloriously naked presence had wiped her thoughts clean—well, not clean, exactly—and she hadn't moved to remove her own pants. But he was on the job, handy as always, grabbing the fabric around her hips and jerking them with her panties down her legs and over her ankles. Her breasts jiggled around with the movement, which did seem to confuse him for a second, but he plowed on heroically, and soon they were both naked.

He climbed on top of her. He'd already opened a condom. "Billie," he said hoarsely.

"Ian."

He kissed her hard on the mouth, then moved back a few inches and looked into her eyes. "You're sure?"

She nodded. "You?"

His expression darkened. She felt his hand slide up her thigh and push her legs apart. And then his fingers were everywhere, stroking her, discovering how wet she was.

"This is for me," he said, breathing hard as he caressed her.

She arched her back, pressing into his palm, tired of waiting. "Do it."

"Ask nicely." He wasn't smiling.

"Please," she said through her teeth. He was touching her, sliding in and out but not deeply enough, not nearly. Torture.

He pressed his mouth against hers, his tongue moving between her lips and opening her the same way his fingers were invading her below, and in spite of the inadequacy of these gestures, she began to feel the tightening, spiraling start of her climax.

"Now," she gasped, writhing under him. She didn't want it to end too soon.

Did he want her to beg? She could do that. Pride had never held her back. But then she realized he'd only paused to put on the condom, and she stopped herself from helping, not wanting to highlight her expertise in that area.

The next moment, he lifted his weight, settled on top of her, and thrust inside her.

Filled her.

Oh.

"Billie," he groaned.

Was that her name? She lifted her knees and took him deeper, however dangerous that seemed at the moment. He was huge.

With another groan, he began moving inside her, leaning forward to kiss her cheek, her ear, her eyebrow, her nose. "I'll try to make this last."

"Don't," she said, grabbing his ass, stroking his thick, muscled thigh. "Just do it. Do it. Fuck me, Ian."

"God," he said roughly, shuddering in her arms.

"Harder," she whispered.

"You're going to kill me." But his next thrust nearly split her in half. "Oh, my God."

They stopped talking. He pounded into her, hard and wild, the way she wanted it. She wanted him as out of control as she was. Yes. Yes. More. They were wordless, they said everything. Their bodies were slick and hot, joining and fighting one another.

The flimsy bed knocked against the wall, faster and faster. She dug her nails into his powerful shoulders, squeezed him inside her, dared him to give and take it all. He met her challenge, riding the wave, shoving his hand between their bodies to make her splinter and spiral and finally, with him shuddering inside her, fall over the crest into happy, sweet, mindless release.

Chapter 27

AFTER A FEW minutes, Ian's heart returned to its normal rhythm, and he felt like he might be able to breathe properly in another five.

Billie was motionless beneath him, her eyes closed. He was still inside her, but knew he couldn't stay there or the condom would slip off.

She was probably on the pill, but he imagined what a pregnancy would mean for them and their families. Billie had been afraid to tell Jane about him fixing up the house; news that he'd impregnated her would be slightly more intimidating. She might leave the country rather than face her sister with that bombshell.

Kissing her pretty eyebrow, he withdrew and went to the bathroom, where his small shop towel hung still over the shower curtain rod.

He was glad he hadn't gone home for a shower. If he had, he didn't think he'd be here now.

The doorbell rang, reminding him he'd ordered dinner for them a little while ago, back when he'd thought it would be delivered before what they'd just done, not after.

Well, damn. Here he was, stuck in the bathroom naked again.

This time without even his dirty clothes to cover himself.

The bell rang again, but soon he heard Billie's friendly voice and then the door banging shut. He'd have to pay her back for dinner. The restaurant he'd chosen wasn't cheap, and he'd ordered a feast.

To his surprise, even though the door had closed, he heard a man's voice and then Billie's again.

Ian eyed the shop towel, estimating its square footage. Not nearly enough to cover nearly enough of him.

He waited, straining to hear what was happening in the hallway. They didn't come closer but continued talking near the front door.

Finally he heard the door slam shut again. And a few seconds later, Billie's voice just outside the bathroom.

"Coast is clear," she said, sounding amused. Then she mumbled something.

He opened the door, taking in the delicious sight of her wearing his T-shirt over her jeans. "What did you say?"

"Nothing." Her eyes twinkled. "Guess who that was?"

"No, you said something. What was it?"

Eyes darting to one side, she lifted a hand to her hair and twirled a curly strand around her finger. "I said, 'unlike before.'"

He frowned, thinking over the exact words. "You saw me."

She nodded, twirling the hair more furiously. "You called my name."

"You didn't answer."

"I came out to see what you wanted." Her gaze lowered. "You were facing the other way."

"I needed a towel."

"I'm not sure about that."

He grinned, catching her around the waist. His shirt made her even sexier than usual. "Why didn't you say anything?"

"I hadn't decided yet what I was going to do."

"What finally helped you decide?" He nuzzled her neck, caressing her breast, dragging his thumb over the nipple until it puckered. "It was my ass, wasn't it?"

"Don't joke. I told you I was weak."

Hearing the faint sadness in her voice, he drew back to see her face. "You're amazing," he said.

"You didn't ask me who was at the door."

"Wasn't it the food?"

"No. It was Todd."

He must've stared at her uncomprehendingly.

"From next door," she continued. "The cat guy."

His hold on her tightened. The guy had come inside for a while. "What did he want?"

"I'm not sure. He seemed like he was complaining about the debris box and the storage unit and your truck taking up all the parking spaces," she said. "But then he asked me out on a date."

"What did you say?"

"Well, I figured we'd be done here by eight, so he's coming over then." She captured his nipple between her little fingers and twisted. When he doubled over, laughing through the pain, she added, "It would be better if you got dressed before he gets here. I don't want him to feel uncomfortable."

He grabbed her wrist and pulled her close, happier than he'd felt in a long time. "Smartass," he said, kissing her.

The doorbell rang again.

"Finally," he said. "That should be the Indian food." He caught the bottom of his T-shirt and pulled it over her head, not willing to greet the delivery guy without it. Then he jogged into the bedroom for his jeans and credit card.

When he went to the front door, she was peeking out at him from the bathroom. "Don't be surprised if Todd asks you to leave," she said. "You make the cat nervous."

He laughed again. She always made him laugh.

It was not Todd, thank God, but their dinner, and in moments the entire house was filled with the spicy, savory scent of curry. His stomach growled, reminding him he'd had a long day of hard labor, followed by some of the hottest sex of his life, without a decent meal.

She joined him in the kitchen wearing her own shirt again, her cheeks pink, her brown hair loose and mussed, her eyes warm.

As he sat her at the chair next to him, she glanced up, just a glance, and smiled into his eyes for a quick moment before reaching for her glass. He froze, feeling his heart squeeze in his chest like a peach caught in a cast-iron bench vise.

"This looks amazing," she said, audibly inhaling as she looked into the half-dozen containers one by one. "Where's yours?"

When he didn't laugh, she turned to look at him.

"What's wrong?" she asked.

The handle on the vice turned another ninety degrees. He managed to smile at her.

"Nothing," he said lightly, kissing her on the forehead. "Let's eat."

...

Billie woke up in the dark with her cheek pressed against Ian's chest. In fact, from the sticky feel under her face, she was pretty sure she'd been drooling on it in her sleep.

How appropriate. He was delicious.

Wiping her lips with the back of her hand, and using the corner of the bedsheet to delicately pat his damp chest hair, she squinted at the clock near the bed. 3:41. A siren wailed in the distance, fading as it passed.

"Morning," Ian said.

She dropped the sheet, startled by his deep voice. "I thought you were asleep."

"You were drooling over me. I thought I might get lucky."

"Actually," she said, "I was drooling *on* you. There's a difference."

"Now you tell me." He reached down and pulled her on top of him, his powerful arms lifting her easily before his hands began roving over her body again.

Drowsy, she bumped her chin against his jaw, kissed it to make it better, found his mouth there instead, and spent the next few minutes making out while she was half-asleep. After dinner, they'd made love again, longer and slower than they had the first time, and she'd only fallen asleep a couple of hours ago. In other words, she was tired, and even his kisses couldn't keep her awake anymore.

He pulled the sheet, which had fallen to one side, over her shoulders, then caressed her through the thin fabric. Lying on top of him made her a little uncomfortable, in part because her breasts were large and round and tilted her sideways, ruining her balance, and also because she could hear the hitch in his breathing from supporting her weight. But she decided he'd inform her if he was dying, and went limp.

"I have to go," he said right as she was drifting off into a very nice dream about him French-kissing her over a plate of tandoori chicken.

No, she was just remembering something that had actually happened. She knew what her favorite dish at an Indian restaurant was going to be from now on.

Until everything crashed and burned, that is, and her heart was broken and Jane refused to talk to her again. Then she'd have to order something like the spinach dish that tasted good but looked like baby poo.

"Your sister is coming first thing in the morning, isn't she?" he asked.

Chapter 28

WITH A GROAN, Billie rolled off Ian's chest, careful not to unman him as she did so, and flopped onto her back at his side. The bed didn't have room for both of them, and her right butt cheek hung off the edge of the mattress.

It was best for him to go home, if just so they could get some sleep.

"Yeah, she said she'd be here at eight." She felt her butt cheek slip off another inch. "I'm not sure if she's kidding."

"Probably shouldn't risk it," he said.

As if they hadn't risked it already. As if they could ever go back to the way they were before.

"Probably shouldn't." She tried to roll gracefully out of the bed, instead falling onto her hands and knees with her big beautiful butt in the air and a stray fragment of plywood embedded in her kneecap.

He must've heard her pained intake of breath, because he climbed out and knelt beside her. "What happened?"

"Just a splinter." She pinched it between her fingernails and plucked it out. "It'll be nice when the floors are finished."

"Just say the word," he said.

"Word."

Chuckling, he lifted her with him to their feet. "I'll call the contractor."

She realized then she'd gotten carried away. "No, wait. I'll need to talk to Jane. We're going to make a budget. We can't afford to do everything at once."

"Billie," he said, stroking the hair away from her face. "You don't have to worry about that."

It was dark and his hands felt good, but she came wide awake. "Just because I slept with you doesn't mean you're going to take over my life."

He dropped his hands and took a step back. She suddenly felt the chill in the room. It was still February, and the night was cold.

Maybe her tone had been sharper than she'd intended. Rubbing her upper arms, she said, "I mean, I can't take your money."

"My money." He said it as if the words tasted bad.

"I'd feel weird about it."

"I'm not offering because we slept together," he said. "You've got to know that."

She did. She knew. "It doesn't really matter what I think. What would I tell Jane?"

"I could talk to her," he said. "We're old friends. Maybe she wouldn't have a problem with it. She's cool with me doing the work, which actually costs me more than paying someone else to do it. Lost hours at the office add up. She'll see the logic of it."

The reminder of what he was giving them, time or money, didn't make her feel better. "But I won't."

In the darkness, she thought she felt him smile. "No, you're not as logical."

She didn't want him talking to Jane. It was bad enough they'd

Facing her sister in a few hours wasn't going to be easy. "Are you going to leave or what? I'm naked and I'm freezing."

"I'm finding it difficult to leave," he said, cupping her left breast and sucking the nipple into his mouth. Delicious sensations shot down her belly and her body informed her she was ready for more lovemaking in spite of her exhaustion.

In the end, he was the one to break away. After a final caress and suckle, he straightened, kissed her on the lips, and tried to guide her back down to the bed. "Sleep. Don't see me to the door."

She wiggled past him and bent over to get the quilt. Wrapping it around her shoulders, she moved to the doorway, stepping lightly to avoid any other shrapnel. "I'll need to lock up after you."

They were both probably remembering the disagreement about the keys. This time, though, he didn't argue. "Of course. Make sure you turn the deadbolt," he said before he put on his shoes and left her to sleep the rest of the night alone.

...

But Jane didn't show up at eight. It was pushing noon when Billie, going through a box of papers in the second bedroom as she sipped her third mug that morning of strong black tea, heard the front door open.

Billie had been up and ready for painting for three hours now and was irritated with Jane for not coming earlier. She'd ignored Billie's texts, too. These were precious hours she could've been sleeping.

She finished her tea and looked into the empty cup. No, she probably wouldn't have been sleeping. Since Ian had left, the slightest noise or chill or bump in the mattress had kept her awake, worrying about her sister, her job, her life in general.

She'd done it again. Given in to lust. But this time she'd jumped into bed with a man whose life was intertwined with her family, a person she'd always appreciated having as a friend because he was smart, interesting, and helpful.

Helpful. Ugh. He'd offered to pay for everything. He was already putting in time and sweat, roping in minions with promises of priceless investment advice, and acting as general contractor, just because he wanted to.

And she didn't know what they'd do without him. She'd probably still be sleeping in the kitchen on a camp mattress, the other rooms filled with garbage and cat litter, the floor encased in rotting carpet, and with all the stress at work, she'd probably be on the verge of giving up the house and finding a new apartment. In New Hampshire.

Was she using him? Maybe she was no better than her ex-boyfriend. Worse if you factored in the traitorous sister element. A lowering thought. She hadn't thought she could get any lower unless she dug a hole in the ground.

But she'd promised Ian she wouldn't regret it. And she didn't. Once he'd kissed her, it had been inevitable. If she was honest with herself, the only thing keeping them apart was his lack of interest. She'd always—not consciously, but down there in the plumbing, so to speak—she'd wanted him. To her, he'd always be the smartest, kindest, best-looking, most talented guy she'd ever known personally. Impressions from adolescence could last a lifetime. She was like a baby duck, and he'd imprinted on her at a critical moment in development.

"Billie?" Jane's voice reached her from the hall.

"Back here." She dug her hand into the box and pulled out an old newspaper clipping of a *Cathy* cartoon that joked about hoarding boxes of old papers. It was very meta.

"Hey," Jane said.

Something about her voice made Billie jerk around. When she saw her sister, she dropped the cartoon and bolted to her feet. "What happened?"

Jane hadn't brushed her hair. Neither a swipe of mascara nor dab of lip gloss enhanced her features. And she wore yoga pants and a hoodie, which for her was like Billie wearing fishnet hot pants and a bra with nipple tassels: she might like to wear them now and then, but not out of the house.

Did she *know*? Billie's pulse kicked up a notch. She was stupid to think she could hide anything from her sister, and a terrible person for even trying.

It was good Jane knew. They shouldn't keep secrets from each other. Was hot sex more important than family? Of course not. Billie had finally gone too far. This wasn't flunking algebra for the third time. This was her relationship with her sister.

"Are you all right?" Billie asked, twining her hands together in front of her.

Jane sighed. "Ask Mom. She'll tell you."

Chapter 29

BILLIE'S STOMACH TURNED inside out. "*Mom?*" This was the price of sleeping with the son of her mother's best friend. "How did she know?" Billie whispered, afraid she might vomit.

"I'm sorry, I should've told you first," Jane said, rubbing her face with both hands. She stayed there for a moment, a classic posture of grief. Then she looked up. "But I knew you'd always hated Andrew. I wasn't ready to hear you be happy it was over."

Jane's words flowed over Billie like cold rain on a grass fire.

Andrew. She was talking about Andrew.

Thank God. She felt the tension leaving her body. Her heartbeat began to slow down.

But her relief only proved to her again what a terrible person she was.

"I moved out last night and drove up to Mom's," Jane continued. "This house isn't ready for more clutter. I managed to fit everything except my furniture into the van. I'm going back for that today."

"You always were a minimalist."

"Thus the minivan," Jane said, managing a weak smile.

It was an old joke. Jane didn't have many possessions, even before she'd read that Japanese book about getting rid of things